W9-CAZ-387

To MARLENE,

Thank you ; enjoy!.

Scott BAKER Sweeney

THE TEARS OF MARY

SCOTT BAKER SWEENEY

Bloomington, IN Milton Keynes, UK

authorHOUSE®

AuthorHouse™
1663 Liberty Drive, Suite 200
Bloomington, IN 47403
www.authorhouse.com
Phone: 1-800-839-8640

AuthorHouse™ *UK Ltd.*
500 Avebury Boulevard
Central Milton Keynes, MK9 2BE
www.authorhouse.co.uk
Phone: 08001974150

First published by AuthorHouse 10/18/2007

ISBN: 978-1-4343-0607-4 (sc)
ISBN: 978-1-4343-0608-1 (hc)

Library of Congress Control Number: 2007902372

Printed in the United States of America
Bloomington, Indiana

This book is printed on acid-free paper.

FROM THE BOOK OF KELLS

Better far the praise of men.

Tis to sit with book and pen.

Pangur bears me no ill-will; he too plies his simple skill

Written by Irish Monks

CHAPTER 1:

ACCORDING TO JOHN

Standing near the cross was Jesus's mother, Mary; his aunt; and Mary Magdalene. It was Friday about nine o'clock in the morning when the crucifixion began. About noon, darkness fell across the entire land, lasting until three o'clock that afternoon. Jesus shouted, "Eli. Eli Lama Sabachtani," which means, "My God, my God, why have you forsaken me?" Then Jesus shouted out again, dismissed his spirit, and died.

Afterward Joseph of Arimathed and Nicodemus (close friends of Jesus) took Jesus's body down and took it away. Together they wrapped Jesus's body in a long linen cloth saturated with spices, as was the custom of the Jewish people before the burial. The place of the crucifixion was near a grove of trees, where there was a new tomb that had never been used before. This is where they laid Jesus. Then they rolled a large stone across the entrance.

Early Sunday morning, while it was still dark, Mary Magdalene came to the tomb and found that the stone was rolled aside.

Mary ran and found Simon, Paul, and John (disciples of Jesus). "They have taken the Lord's body out of the tomb and I don't know where they have put him!" Peter, Simon, and John ran back to the tomb and saw the linen cloth laying there but no Jesus. Until then the disciples had not realized that the scriptures said Jesus would come to life again! The men then went home. And by the time Mary had returned to the tomb and was standing outside crying. As she wept, she stopped and looked in and saw white-robed angels sitting at the head and food of the place where the body of Jesus had been lying.

"Why are you crying?" the angels asked her.

"Because they have taken away my Lord," she replied, "and I don't know where they have put him."

She then glanced over her shoulder and saw someone standing behind her. It was Jesus but she didn't recognize him. "Why are you crying?" he asked her. "Who are you looking for?"

Mary thought he was the gardener, so she said, "If you have taken him away, tell me where you have put him and I will go get him."

"Mary!" Jesus said.

She turned to him. "MASTER!"

CHAPTER 2:

The relevance of the event, which occurred two thousand years ago, will begin to make sense once you hear my strange, bizarre story. My father used to tell me that everyone in life has some sort of purpose and that things happen for a reason. As a young man I never grasped exactly what he was talking about, but believe me, I do now.

Let me first start by telling you some things about me. My name is Austin Brock. I'm a recently retired U.S. Navy Seal. Strangely my formal education is in religious studies from Notre Dame University.

Growing up in a small farming community in central Indiana as a child, my dreams of the future went only as far as the stalks of corn that I could see past. The Brock family was a humble, religious, hard-working family, typical of the 1970's.

Our mornings started at 5:30, when we started shoveling silage for the cattle, followed by corn meal for the hogs. During the afternoons, my brother and I were in the fields disking or planting, whichever the season demanded.

God bless my mother! She insisted on the family attendance at our kitchen table for three meals a day. The entire family, including grandparents, were not allowed to be AWOL. Consequently each meal would begin with a prayer of thanks.

Work around our small farm was hard 365 days of the year. The only break was of course Sunday mornings in church.

Unlike my brothers, farming was not my passion. I dreamed of adventure. I would read anything and everything I could get a hold of and daydream for hours afterward about what I'd just read.

When it was time for me to graduate high school, I knew that there was only one option if I ever wanted to get off the farm. It was college. Don't get me wrong; I love the farm, my family, and my friends. I just felt there was something more for me than the 260-acre farm could provide.

My mother must have been reading my mind; she knew that perhaps farming wasn't for me, and she was highly instrumental as well as influential when talking my father into letting me go to college. She always had a knack of imposing her will on my father without him even suspecting. I remember him saying, like it was his idea all along, "Maybe, mother, it's time we let Austin leave the farm and sow his wild oats." How funny was that. Going away to study religion at college was my father's idea of sowing wild oats.

Notre Dame was an easy choice. My grades were good enough and it was a Catholic school (the only Catholic school, according to my father). It was also a close drive from home, so I could come home on the weekends to help on the farm. But the most important part of this formula was that I got accepted!

I won't bore you with most of my college life; however, my introduction to my roommate sent me sailing toward an entirely new dimension in my life.

CHAPTER 3:

The year was 1987, the day, August 18, a day that will live in infamy—well, at least in my own mind. It was moving day and I was moving into my dorm. The school had pre-selected my roommate at my request, and he turned out to be an exchange student from Ireland.

"Top of the morning to ya," said a voice flowing out from behind a large piece of plastic. This voice was attempting to hang some makeshift shower curtain over the only window of our modest dorm room.

"Good morning," I replied. "I'm Austin Brock."

My roommate must be a shower curtain, I thought to myself and laughed. Out from behind a gaudy, flowered plastic cloth appeared a red-headed guy wearing a large grin from ear to ear.

"Pleased to make your acquaintance. I'm Tommy O'Shea from Dublin, Ireland. I just arrived yesterday. Never been to the United States, let alone South Bend, Indiana. I thought I'd try to shine up the place before you **arrived**. I understand, Austin, you're a farmer too."

"Yes I am, or at least my **family here** is," I said, nodding at my mom and dad.

Shaking the hands of my parents, who were looking on, Tommy continued, "We have a large potato farm and raise sheep just outside of Dublin. Being the oldest of four children, it was decided that I would study business in one of America's great universities. Hopefully I might bring back some knowledge as to better manage our family businesses."

With all that unsolicited information, I looked over at my mom as she looked back at me with a smile. I could tell she already knew that Tommy and I would hit it off, and she was right. From that moment on we were basically inseparable.

CHAPTER 4:

Other than our farming background, we were as different as night and day. Even our appearances were different. I am tall six foot three, weigh 220 pounds, and have sandy-blonde hair and green eyes. Tommy is of a shorter stature. He is five foot six (in shoes), weighs 160 pounds, and has short red hair and Irish blue eyes.

I like short girls; he likes tall. I would rather go fishing or go on a run. He would rather play chess or watch TV. I like American football; he likes European football. I like REM; he listens to the Cranberries. Well, you get the picture.

Tommy was also partial to shots: Jameson's Irish whiskey chased with a pint of Guinness (What else?). When Tommy started drinking, his thick Irish brogue became thicker. I myself found it more interesting to be a spectator than participate in his binges. Of course, at the time, I hadn't reached the legal drinking age.

By our third year we were still roommates. Only now we were sharing an apartment just off campus. I was able to bring Tommy around to my kind of fun. I convinced him that fighting Irish football games were the place to be, especially if afterward we could parlay that fun into post-game parties.

Not all of our fun involved sixty thousand other fans. Occasionally we would opt for a more relaxed afternoon and go fishing; however, it was mandatory that we took along two extremely cute coeds, one short and one tall.

There's one thing I haven't mentioned about Tommy. The O'Sheas aren't just your average Irish potato farmers. No indeed. They are an extremely wealthy Irish family. They reside in their sixteenth-century castle, built by his ancestors. The O'Sheas fought the English for the retention of their land in the tenth and seventeenth centuries and probably would have lost it to the Brits if it weren't for the fact that one of the young "Randy" O'Shea males wound up impregnating one of the royal family's young lassies.

The king of England was so embarrassed by what had happened that he allowed the two kids to secretly marry and the O'Shea clan to keep their land and continue farming. To maintain this secret disgrace, the young princess was forbidden to return into English society. Even from her royal-blooded family she was banished. The O'Sheas were warned never to publicly speak of this or they would lose their land along with their heads.

Tommy had a knack for story telling. He said "weaving yarns" was maybe the only inheritance he would get from his family. Tommy claimed that all his kin from Ireland were all good story tellers, and I believe him.

Telling tales and passing on folklore is most likely what families like the O'Sheas had been spending their evenings doing for centuries. Tommy told me they didn't get a TV until 1980. This forced them into story telling along with reading for their only entertainment.

Most of Tommy's yarns started out with me asking him about something regarding my studies, and suddenly a story evolved, sometimes lasting into the wee hours of the morning. Don't get me wrong; I was always totally consumed. I hung on to every adjective or verb that flowed off his tongue.

The irony of this school thing is I was very good in business and economics, and Tommy wasn't. We should've swapped majors but didn't; however, we both helped each other out tremendously.

My last year of school consisted of a whirlwind. It was a jam-packed studying marathon just so we could graduate in May.

I was writing a paper on Mary Magdalene for one of my upper-level classes and was struggling with coming up with a theory about what became of Mary after the crucifixion. As always, I asked Tommy for his input.

CHAPTER 5:

"Hey, O'Shea, what do you know about Mary Magdalene?"

The following four words from Tommy returned to me as fast as a prize fighter's reflex: "The tears of Mary!"

"What was that?" I said?

"Oh nothing, Austin. No, I suppose I know not much more than what you can read in the Bible."

"Well, what did you mean when you said 'the tears of Mary'?" I asked again.

"Oh, Austin, I really can't elaborate. I shouldn't have even spoken out."

"Hey, hold on. When has Tommy O'Shea ever not spoken out or elaborated on any subject?"

"Oh well. What the hell! Get me my bottle of Jameson's behind the bookshelf and two glasses. And by the way, I hope you don't expect to make your early class tomorrow morning."

The reason I am reluctant about telling you this story is because its been for the most part a secret in my family for years—centuries in fact. And this is not just the case in my family the O'Sheas. A select few families or clans in Europe and other parts of the Christian community in the Middle East know of this story.

The story Tommy was about to tell eventually turned into print and became part my final essay, and that essay would come at a great cost.

"Well, lad, as you know," Tommy started, "Mary Magdalene was a devoted disciple and friend to Jesus. She was aiding and caring for them during their travels. Jesus had saved her from her wretched ways and because of this she dedicated her life to Jesus and God until the end of her physical stay here on Earth."

As the bible reports, Mary was a present at the crucifixion and went to the tomb two days later, on Sunday. The scriptures said that she was the first to arrive at Jesus's tomb. Mary witnessed that the large stone that had blocked the entrance was rolled away and Jesus's body was gone.

Mary was totally engulfed by the anguish of losing a loved one. This hit her like a large cold wave from the sea. Her strength was gone, and Mary's emotions were uncontrollable. She sobbed heavily into her scarf, soaking her garment completely. She cried until a mellow voice projected out from the dark tomb. This was the voice of an angel asking her. 'Why do you cry, Mary'?

"Well, you know the story," commented Tommy.

Mary ran away to tell the others, clinging to her soaked scarf.

Mary's uncontrollable grief was replaced with excitement. She ran into her humble dwelling. She shared the story with other family members—a cousin, her cousin's husband, and their children. She paid little attention to her tear-soaked garment, not realizing that it was still strangely very wet even though by that time several hours had gone by.

Mary quickly folded it away and placed it on a shelf above her bed to deal it with later. What she had just experienced that day caused her to become very fatigued, to the point that she laid down to take a nap.

Mary fell into a deep sleep that lasted for several hours into the night. Suddenly she was awakened by a soft voice calling her name.

When she opened her eyes, the voice said, "Mary, do not be afraid." The voice belonged to the angel that Mary recognized from Jesus's tomb earlier that day. "I have brought you a gift of love and devotion from your savior and friend, Jesus. This gift of great beauty and pure brilliant light resembles the light that shines through the entrance gate of heaven. This brilliant gift represents purity and love and can never be embraced or coveted by evil or impurity." With this, the angel was gone and Mary fell back to sleep until the next evening.

Mary awoke to the sound of tapping raindrops on the leaves of the fig tree outside of her window. She rose in bed, still fully dressed from the day before, when she lay down to nap.

She suddenly realized she had slept for quite some time but didn't immediately remember her visit from the angel. Mary walked over to the window to close the shutters. As she reached out to grab the latch, the memory of her visitor filled her mind. *I must have been dreaming?* she thought to herself.

Closing the shutter, Mary continued on with her morning grooming and chores; however, she was totally consumed by the thoughts of her experience yesterday and the surreal visit or dream she'd had during her nap. After helping her cousin with breakfast, she decided to gather her garments to wash them at the river once the rain had stopped.

Mary reached up to grab the scarf she had placed on the shelf the day before and noticed that it was budging out as if it was filled with loaves of bread. When she went to pick it up, the weight surprised her.

Falling back to the bed, still clinging to the scarf, Mary inquisitively pondered the notion of what was in her once tear-soaked scarf. Out from behind the folded cloth peered brilliant beams of white and blue light shooting out like fiery stars.

"Oh my!" she screamed, the brilliant light momentarily blinding her as well as taking away her breath. It was the most beautiful vision Mary's eyes had ever seen.

She stretched her garment out. It practically took up her entire bed. She was now staring wide-eyed and open-mouthed at a sparkling large mound of perfectly symmetrical gems— diamonds in fact. Mary had never seen diamonds that close, let alone been able to touch them.

Tommy paused. "Austin, I'm not boring you, am I?" he said teasingly. Tommy looked like he was starting to feel the effects of the Jamison's. He had been stopping to take sips periodically.

"Shut up! And continue O'Shea," I snapped.

"All right, all right". Tommy grunted.

"Well, you can image Mary was in shock after what happened a few days earlier with the crucifixion of Jesus and then his resurrection from the tomb, the visit from the angel, and now this," Tommy continued.

"Still staring at this large pile of radiant beauty, Mary raked the diamonds back into a consolidated mound more to the center of her scarf. Mary's heart was as pure as the raindrops outside of her window. When she looked at the magnitude of gems, she saw great beauty and warmth, a precious gift from her savior.

"What she did not see or feel was wealth or greed; I think Jesus realized the diamonds would not affect Mary negatively. This is why he chose this gift for her; she would look to these diamonds with complete reverence.

"However, the ugly truth was these hundreds of stones were worth a vast fortune that would equal the spoils of any Roman king.

"To put in perspective of magnitude of these diamonds, Mary made reference to the overall weight of this bounty to be about the weight of four medium-size fieldstones.

"Austin, I would guess, oh, about thirty or forty U.S. pounds worth of precious diamonds. It goes without saying that these crystallized carbon rocks were worth a king's ransom.

"Searching for something to store her gift in, Mary selected a clay pot, or urn, usually reserved for collecting water for bathing. She gathered in the corners of her garment. With all her might, she lifted the fabric nearly to the point of it ripping. She then placed the weighted bundle down into the pot.

"It was nearly twelve years before Mary mentioned this gift to anyone—not even to her family or the disciples. To Mary, this sacred gift was private. She would look at these diamonds almost every day. Sometimes she would, with all her might, pull the scarf bundle, all thirty-five pounds or so, out of the clay pot, displaying them over her entire bed. Other days she would just peer down into the pot, admiring the pure beauty.

"Mary revealed to her family later in her life that when she would look into the glow of the diamonds it would feel like it did when she used to look into Jesus's eyes.

"Austin, as I said earlier, it was several years before Mary told anyone of her most precious gift, but she was getting older now and was still living in Jerusalem with her cousin and her cousin's husband and their family.

"Mary began suffering from a crippling illness and she felt her time left on Earth was short. So she deiced to tell her cousin, Martha, and her husband, Paul, of her precious gift.

"Mary let them know her intent after her passing was to be buried with her diamonds; however, her wishes were not carried out. Paul and Martha had lived a normal, faithful life. Both had been baptized and were basically good people.

"But the temptation of greed overwhelmed them both."

CHAPTER 6:

When Mary finally passed, her body was taken to the nearby temple. The customary Jewish ceremonies were performed and she was prepared and taken to her tomb for her burial. The ugliness of greed now consumed Paul and Martha during the entire ceremony. Instead of grief for their older cousin, they were filled with thoughts of their assumed great wealth and couldn't wait to return home to access their newfound riches. But something happened that they were not counting on.

When Paul and Martha returned home, Paul retrieved the pot to examine their wealth. The clay pot seemed very light compared to normal. (Paul had been the one to help Mary on several occasions lift the pot so she could view the diamonds.) Something was very wrong. Paul hastily reached in and pulled out Mary's scarf. It was soaking wet, but there were no diamonds. Paul and Martha's first thoughts were that someone had stolen her diamonds even though they were the only ones to know of their existence. Suddenly they both fell to their knees, stricken down by extreme grief and shame. It was such a horrible feeling, like someone has stuck a cold steel stake right through their hearts.

Paul and Marta's souls left their bodies; this allowed them to see clearly what they had done—the true awfulness of how they had behaved. How could they live with themselves? How could they be capable of what they had just done—the lying, the deceit, and the greed!

CHAPTER 7:

"All this agony seemed to last an eternity, what I would guess to be like meeting Saint Peter, one judgment day."

Tommy continued by explaining that when their souls finally returned to their bodies, Paul and Martha placed the wet scarf back into the pot and hurryingly took it back to the temple to have the attendant place it back with Mary in her tomb, per her wishes.

Paul and Martha returned back home not realizing the miracle that had occurred. Once the pot was inside the tomb, safe with Mary Magdalene's corpse, the tears transformed back into precious gems.

Many years passed before Mary's tomb was opened again.

Grave robbers looking for anything they would be able to sell happened upon her tomb. They removed the sealed entrance and, while ravaging through her belongings, realized her name, Mary Magdalene.

"Could this be the same Mary Magdalene who assisted Jesus as in the scripture writings of hundred years earlier?" announced one thief to another. "She has no monetary value, no wealth. She was merely and old peasant woman."

"Yes, but what about articles of clothing? Or surely her belongings might have some worth."

The belongings of Mary Magdalene would bring a pretty coin or two.

Seeing the clay pot next to the cloth-wrapped body, they peered down into the opening and pulled out a heavily soaked scarf. Miraculously the scarf was in good shape for its age. So the thieves left with the pot and its content.

Once out of the tomb, the two men were struck by the same thing that Paul and Martha had experienced many years prior. They never knew that the clay pot and scarf they stole was basically a chalice filled with priceless diamonds for many years before they entered the tomb.

Once again the swift sword of anguish struck down another victim. This time it was the tomb robbers. Their souls left their bodies and when their souls returned the men immediately dropped all their loot (almost all their loot) and ran away clinging tightly onto the clay pot, not knowing why, but they knew they had to expedite this clay pot as far away as possible.

What the thieves did not realize was that from that point on they were not in control of their actions. A higher power was directing their journey.

They were totally consumed with getting this clay pot from Jerusalem to the Mediterranean Sea. The men traveled for hours without stopping for even a drink of water. Their destination was Haifa, a port city with heavy merchant travel mostly from Africa to Rome. There the men waited by the sea for days, just sitting, waiting, watching the ships load and unload their cargo. What or who they were waiting on they did not know. "I don't believe they even questioned that in their minds," added Tommy. On the fourth day as the sun rose, the crew of a smallish sailing vessel was beginning to remove their tethered lines. A few men were loading their belonging onto the boat when one man in particular caught the thieves' eyes. They rose to their feet and ran over to greet the man.

"Sir, sir" one of the thieves said, crying out for his attention. "We know not who you are; nor do we know where you are going. We only know we are to give you this clay pot and it's belongings for your safekeeping and delivery."

The weathered man of the sea was dressed in a tattered cloth jacket that hung to the top of his worn boots.

"You men can call me Jebadia; I am the captain of this sailing craft. We are bound for Crete then onto Sardinia and finally France. Do you men wish to retain my services?"

Tommy stretched his arms, saying, "Austin, I need to divert away momentarily to tell you something. Please keep in mind I'm telling you this story as close to the same way my father told me and my grandfather told him. Obviously the names of cities and countries are as they are today, not as they were in the early centuries, as to better understand the geography. Back to the story."

The men reached out and presented Jebadia with the clay pot. With a puzzled look on Jeb's face, he reached inside the pot and pulled out a very wet scarf. The garment looked like and had the smell of a very old cloth.

"What is this and why is it wet?" barked Jebadia.

"We cannot answer any questions other than it's a garment which belonged to Mary Magdalene, friend to Jesus of Nazareth, mentioned in the scripture."

Jeb did not hear what the two had just said. Upon his touching of the scarf, he instantly knew all the facts others intended him to know. His own tears were now flowing down his face. After putting the sacred garment back into the pot, he carefully picked up the pot and carried it on board.

"Well, Austin, now Mary's scarf was on its journey."

CHAPTER 8:

Several months of passage went by for Jeb's small sailing craft, trekking the Mediterranean Sea. Their tiring journey led them around Crete on to Sicily and Sardinia, and finally to Lerins, France.

"Austin, me story is making me quite weary, we've drank all the Jameson and the night is turning into dawn. I've talked and you've listened all night. Soon you will be just as tired, but I will bear the guilt of passing on this secret to a non-family member, worse a non-Irishmen."

"If you stop now, Tommy, I'll kill you!" I pleaded, "Please continue."

"All right, but I will make this fast. I will speed up by giving you fewer details."

I could tell Tommy was getting very tired and drunk, and I knew he didn't have much more life left in him tonight, but I couldn't let him stop now. I had to know what happed next, so I agreed to accommodate him.

"Just tell me the highlights tonight, Tommy. If I need to, I can always pick your brain later for more details.

"To help me clear my conscience, Austin, I need to make certain you understand that total respect must be given to Mary Magdalene and reverence for her special gift. Complete silence of your knowledge of this event must be maintained as to protect this religious artifact, and the best way to do this is to never repeat these events.

"All right, now, lad, where was I? Ah yes, France."

"Well, Mary's clay pot seemed to be handed off like a baton in a sprinter's race at a track meet. The diamonds traveled from Jerusalem to Lerins via telepathic control over some unsuspecting servants."

Jebadia's immediate focus now was to find the next caretaker of this clay pot, protecting this most precious tear-soaked scarf.

Lerins, France was a small fishing village, but most importantly to this story, Lerins was one of the beginnings of Christianity in Europe. It was a convenient port of landing and final destination point of the Middle East.

CHAPTER 9:

Jebadia found the new caretaker indeed; or should I say the caretaker found Jebadia. He was approached by a young priest studying as a monk at the abbey of Lerins. This young monk named Patrick did not speak a word to Jebadia. He just held out his arms, hugged him, and gave him a kiss on the cheek. Patrick accepted the urn as if he was receiving a lost child, coddling it in his folded arms as he retreated back to the abbey.

Patrick was a poor farm lad from Wales who traveled to Lerins to be trained as a monk. He dreamed of returning to his homeland and perhaps venturing farther to a large island called Ierne. "But I'll get to that later," Tommy added.

Two days before Jebadia landed on the sandy beaches of the south of France, Patrick was visited by Mary's old friend, the angel. The majestic spirit explained to Patrick that he was to receive this great gift that was given to Mary Magdalene by Jesus. This gift of great beauty was to be secured and protected, shrouded with love and purity. "In return the beauty of this gift would be his to behold. You may have already guessed Austin, the scarf was no longer soaked but was filled again with brilliant diamonds. With Patrick they stayed. He did not return to Wales. He did sail over the large island called Ierne, or what I liked to call the emerald island, my home, Ireland.

"One more thing about Patrick, my Indiana friend. You may know of this new caretaker; you Americans celebrate his birthday every March 17th, and later Patrick was given a new first name of Saint. Quoting your American radio celebrity Paul Harvey, 'Now you know the rest of story'."

With that, Tommy rose from his position on the floor, rushed over to his bed, and fell face first into his pillow; there he remained until the early afternoon.

CHAPTER 10:

I'd found it! The theory I'd been searching for. The problem would be I had absolutely no supporting documentation to support it. However, I was so stuck by the story that I lost all my objectivity. I thought this, packaged with my other research, was more than enough to satisfy my final project paper for my religious studies class.

Before Tommy came to life the next day, I started writing down notes; Tommy had drunk most of the whiskey, so I was unaffected by the brown-bottle flu. I knew I had three weeks to gather my thoughts and write this manuscript for submission, so I needed to get started.

I gathered up my things and walked down to the linebacker lounge, a local watering hole. There I secured a table in the corner, where I began to write.

It never occurred to me to let Tommy in on what I was doing, or at least the opportunity never arose to let him know what I was writing about.

I did remember what he has said about the sensitivity of exposing the secret of the diamonds, but I just thought he was over sensationalizing it brought on by the effects of the whiskey he drank. I would have never turned in the paper if I had known it would cause our friendship to end.

I finished my report and turned it in. I was sure that this incredible story would bring me at least a B+. I was so proud I couldn't wait to surprise Tommy with the news. I even went so far as to plan an evening of celebrating with a couple of hot coeds and two bottles of Jameson's, but my plans went very south.

Two days after turning in my report, there was a sealed note handed to me at the doorway of one of my composition classes, informing me of an immediate meeting and requesting my attendance with my religious class teacher, his professor, two priests, and the assistant dean of education.

What a crowd that I was confronted by. Their behavior was almost hostile. They were straight to the point and wanted me to reveal my source. For what they called nonsense. They asked where I got off on taking liberties with a biblical interpretation. Their hostility was very direct. Professor Macquarie was almost humorous as he referred to my report as the "The Dead Cornfield Scrolls." To this day I don't know how I was able to talk my professor into giving me a D instead of an F for that required course, but he did.

Passing grade or not, I was given a negative letter for my student record files. They felt my report was very blasphemous.

Oh yeah, the worst thing was that my parents and Tommy O'Shea, my source, were also sent letters.

My parents were floored. My father thought he has wasted four years of tuition on me just to be humiliated. But the worst thing was Tommy. I thought he was going to kill me, I had never seen him so angry. It was obviously my insensitivity and lack of respect that devastated him. I was also upset and ashamed of what I had done. It was almost as if I had personally taken Mary's tear-soaked scarf and torn it up. I realized that I destroyed our relationship; Tommy could never trust me again. I caused a wound that could never be healed.

Tommy was one third my size in stature, but I remember him pushing me into the door. It felt like I had just been hit by a plow sheer. Tommy said nothing. He just gave me unforgettable look, holding the letter in one hand, crumbling it, and throwing it in my face.

I never spoke to Tommy after that. He moved his things out the next day. I found a check for his portion of the rent along with a brief note telling me of his intent to return home at the end of the semester and not stay for the formal graduation ceremonies. I know it did not sit well with his parents to miss their first son formally receiving his diploma from Notre Dame.

I cannot explain the deep guilt I still feel even today for this totally selfish boneheaded move.

Tommy made good on his word. He did what his note said—or at least it appeared he did. I never saw or heard from him again. I wrote an apology letter a year later and mailed it to his home in Dublin but never received a reply back.

May finally came after four years and lots of memories; now it was time for me to decide what was I going to do with my life. You see, I got my father to pay for my education because my degree was religious studies (which I barely sneaked through), but how was I going to parlay this into earning a living? Becoming celibate and becoming a priest was not an option. This wasn't just something I began thinking about in May; I had been struggling with this issue all year.

One option actually came to me during one of the last football games of the season, the traditional Notre Dame-Navy game. My decision wasn't hard at all, "United States Navy". Obviously religious studies would not help me bypass Annapolis to becoming "naval Brass", but maybe just a degree—any college degree—could help me get accepted into the Seals, which interested me. I would travel, seeing the world, and I could earn enough money to further my education and get into business school.

I was now twenty-three years old, an adult. My parents no longer had legal control over me. My brothers were running the farm, so I wouldn't be missed. So June first I enlisted. Not only did I enlist, I signed up for the Seals.

CHAPTER 11:

In four months I reported to San Diego, California. I went through a brief naval orientation. Then I was off to special forces training, "Buds."

If I joined the Navy and the Seals to punish myself for defrauding Tommy, it worked. It was hell! After my first day, I didn't think I would make it. Running ten miles before 7:00 a.m., heavy exercise and endurance drills, firearm and weapon training, martial arts, classroom studies, water skills, more running. Oh, and then there was the sleep deprivation. I thought I was a good athlete, but I had no idea.

There was no disgrace to dropping out and not completing Buds. Many guys did, some a lot more athletic than me. As the weeks went on I realized that the endurance was more mental than physical and that being physically tough was important but wasn't imperative.

There was a bell at the entrance gate. If you couldn't go through with Buds, all you had to do was ring the bell. You would get your stuff and get reassigned. It was almost too simple. I think that it was another mind test given to the enlistees.

Every day all the guys became tighter and tighter. Going through hell together does create a special bond of trust. When the guy next to you is willing to die to enable the unit to complete the mission, an unbreakable bond forms. The word *comrade* doesn't even come close to describing the relationship. Everyone had nicknames, given to us by our subordinates.

The name given to me was Father Brock. I can't imagine why.

Several weeks of pure hell finally came to an end. Buds was over and I graduated officially as a Navy Seal. For my accomplishments I was very proud. It was probably the proudest moment in my life, more so than graduating from Notre Dame. Even my father agreed, so much so that he placed a *My son is a Navy Seal* sticker on our John Deere combine. I never exactly knew who he expected would see it there. Maybe it was incentive for the rest of my brothers.

I was assigned to a unit, or pod, of eight men, of which five were seasoned veterans of various skills and levels. We were a machine of highly trained individuals. Most deadly as a unit, together we operated like polished gears in a Swiss watch, perfectly meshed to perform flawlessly and with great dependability.

CHAPTER 12:

It was almost unbearable waiting for our first orders. I felt like a caged lion. Every day was like practice for the big game, but the big game never came.

At last my wait was over; my unit flew to Norfolk, Virginia, where we received our orders that placed us on a carrier steaming for the Persian Gulf.

Two weeks later, my flippers were in the dark water of the gulf. I was armed to the teeth with C4 and automatic weapons.

My heart was racing one hundred miles per hour. My brain was a turnstile of all that we had learned in Buds. I kept saying to myself, *Just don't screw up. Just don't screw up.*

From the carrier we joined up with a small fishing boat approximately twenty miles from the coast of Kuwait. This fishing boat just happened to be owned by the CIA. There sure was a lot of fishing going on; there just wasn't any bait, if you catch my drift. This craft took us without much notice to approximately two miles from the Kuwaiti shoreline. There we launched our personal submarines, submerging us in about ten feet of water, and with the shroud of darkness, we hit the water's edge totally undetected. We left our subs underwater, anchored to the sea floor, and buried our wetsuits and tanks in the sand at the beach, to await our return trip.

We camped out on the beach for two days before we were met by undercover intelligence agents of Middle Eastern descent. We were given proper local attire as to blend in, and so we did.

Our orders were strictly reconnaissance. We were to advance to Kuwait City, marking targets for our GPS guided weapons and taking pictures of Iraq's so-called army. To keep our stealth we would lay low during the daylight and move at night.

We were in Kuwait for almost three weeks before any Ranger boots hit the ground. More spectacularly, we watched the first wave of Tomahawks flying overhead and hit their targets dead on—the targets we marked.

Finally our mission was over. We backtracked the same way out as we came in, only our exit was in broad daylight and was a lot faster. The enemy was so preoccupied with our gun ships and jets that filled the sky that they didn't notice us.

This top-secret mission kicked off the shortest war in history. I was extremely proud of myself and my Seal compadres.

I knew most certainly—more so, unquestionably—that becoming a Navy Seal was by far the pinnacle of my life.

Back in the States after the war, I took a ten-day leave, which I spent back home in Indiana, seeing my family and catching up with my friends. I also wrote another letter to Tommy, once again telling him how saddened I was about how our relationship had ended and apologizing for my insensitivity—all this in hopes of earning his forgiveness. I also filled Tommy in on my experiences in Kuwait and how I loved the navy and the Seals.

As I mailed off my letter, I was hoping that Tommy would finally return my letter. Even if he didn't forgive me, I was interested to know how he was doing. I guess I just wanted some closure to this.

After my leave was over, our unit was reassigned to Pearl Harbor, Hawaii. What luck! For the next year our unit did mostly training exercises around the islands of the Pacific, constantly honing our skills and waiting for our next orders.

CHAPTER 13:

It was another day in paradise, with the exception of our ten-mile run, which that day we finished at about 8:00 a.m. I was bent over, clutching my knees after I took a gulp of water. The rest of the guys were breaking up, either heading for the barracks or the showers, when I felt a hand on my shoulder. Thinking it was one of my comrades, I raised from my bent position and blurted out "Now what? After leaving you in my dust during our run, I suppose you want me to kick your ass sparring!" As the word *sparring* left my mouth, I expected to find one of my buds, but to my surprise, instead I found myself staring into the eyes of Lieutenant Commander William Charles, commander of Pearl Harbor naval base.

"Lieutenant Commander, sir!" After giving a quick but direct salute, I said, "Sir, I apologize. I thought—"

"At ease, seaman," ordered Commander Charles.

Glancing over his shoulders, I saw that about fifty feet away was another gentleman dressed in full decorated naval uniform.

Even at a glance I could tell he was very highly ranked. Beside him another man stood looking stoic, wearing a civilian dark blue suit and sunglasses.

"Seaman Brock!"

"Yes sir."

"We were told we could find you here," said the commander. "These men wish to have a word with you, son."

"Of course, sir," I said as I saluted the naval officer. The men turned in unison. The civilian gentleman extended his arm, directing me toward a large black limousine parked about a fifty yards away at the curb.

Inside the limo no words were spoken; not even eye contact was made. There we were: two navy brass members, the man in the suit, and me. The strange event felt as if we were heading for a naval funeral. Then it hit me: "My family. Are they all right?"

"Relax, son, this is not about your family."

For the moment this eased my nerves. We drove to the other side of the base, (the side I rarely saw) the side that was frequented my only dignitaries or high-ranking officers. The limo pulled up to the naval command office. We got out and proceeded inside, down several flights of stairs through guarded doors and long halls, finally arriving at our conference room.

Waiting for us, sitting at a large cherry table, were two more civilian men in suits. As we entered the room, they arose in respect.

"Be seated, gentlemen, and we'll get started."

As lieutenant commander Charles closed the two tall doors, the man in the blue suit took charge.

"Seaman Brock, let us start with introductions. My name is Chief Inspector Kenny, Central Intelligence Agency. The two gentlemen seated when you arrived are special agents Smyth and Gibson, British Intelligence. Of course you know your superiors, Lieutenant Commander Charles and—" Before Kenny could continue, the decorated uniformed gentleman spoke.

"Seaman Brock—what the hell—Austin, I'm Admiral Higgins. Listen, son, Kenny here has some questions he would like to ask you, and perhaps a request. Commander Charles and I are merely here on your behalf and to protect one of our assets. That's you, Brock, or maybe I'll call you Father Brock. Isn't that what they named you at Buds?" the admiral said and laughed.

"Yes sir," I replied inquisitively.

"Well, continue on, Kenny," Higgins requested.

I recall Admiral Higgins's demeanor as being that of Southern gentlemen, or maybe even grandfatherly. But his calming charm never changed the fact that when Admiral Higgins was in a room, he took charge and left no doubt who was in command.

Lieutenant Commander Charles was a tall and thin in stature. I would guess him to be in his mid to upper forties. He had dark brown hair with a few gray streaks. Charles was like most Annapolis graduates; he was total navy and was accustomed to taking and giving orders.

The three intelligence agents, (even though two were from different countries) they were all three the same person, if you know what I mean. Maybe Kenny seemed like more of an asshole. I think maybe that was because he did not possess their British charm and wit or their sterling sharp command of the queen's English. Agent Kenny looked at me and said, "Seamen Brock, I would like to ask you what you know about the tears of Mary."

I remember thinking to myself, *What in the world is he talking about.* Immediately my mind was beginning to be blown by wild thoughts fueled by my anticipation of the unknown. Surely Notre Dame didn't track me down just to continue persecuting me for my stupid paper.

"The tears of Mary, sir? I don't understand."

Kenny continued, "Apparently you wrote a paper in college about the tears of Mary. It caused quite a stir at Notre Dame."

"When you apply to the Seals, your history belongs to the government," Admiral Higgins added. "U.S. Intelligence automatically does a background check. Obviously your college records were reviewed." Higgins smiled. "There apparently was some concern expressed by the higher-ups at the university over your selection of Mary Magdalene as the main character for you paper. However, Seamen Brock, Kenny's cohorts at Central Intelligence found your paper to be quite interesting."

"You see," said Kenny, "it's not your nice little fictional story about Mary's tears that interests us, but instead it's the diamonds. Brock, what we are really interested in is what your paper fails to mention, the exact location in Ireland where these diamonds can be found."

Just then agent Smyth interrupted, "Seamon Brock, or if I may call you Austin, British Intelligence has known for years of the diamonds called the tears of Mary. The myth of where they came from matters little to us. All we have heard is that these thirty or forty U.S. pounds of brilliant flawless diamonds are worth millions and are being protected by monks in a monastery or castle somewhere in Ireland. Up until now, it has only been our business to know of such matters, whether they be myth or truth. Let's just say it's our philosophy that better governments are governments that have no secrets."

CHAPTER 14:

"Obviously our concern is the preservation of the diamonds and keeping them with their rightful owners—that is, of course, if these diamonds really exist and are not some Irish tale. Our problem is if they are not some Irish tale and millions of dollars worth of perfect diamonds are hidden in some monastery protected by monks, and not armed guards, and some evil sorts get their hands on such a bounty, well!" Smyth went on, "We have expressed our concerns to the Irish on several occasions, only to be met with insults, such as British intelligence indeed chasing after a fairy tale, or 'you English need to mind your own matters.' Well, you know of our two countries' wonderfully warm relationship. Believe me, we still have no proof these diamonds even exist, and if they do and they are stolen by some common thieves, then oh well. Not our concern. But on the other hand, if they get stolen by what's left of the Irish Republican Army, or worse yet, Al Qaeda, well then we have a whole new horse of a different color. A bounty like this would go a long way to fund any terrorist organization's efforts."

Agent Gibson continued by saying, "Decades went by without even a peep, until about two months ago when Kenny here contacted us. They have been hearing intelligence chatter from the Middle East the gist of the chatter sounds more like a advertisement written in the *London Times* than something over the Internet or from a cell phone. The frequency of this chatter has increased and goes something like this: a large wealth of diamonds called the tears of Mary is hidden in Europe, more specifically Ireland, and that there would be a large reward offered for these gems if they could be returned to their rightful keeper and not land in the hands of the Christian infidels who had stolen them out of the ancient pyramids. The propaganda was that the diamonds rightfully belonged to the people of Egypt. Oh yes, gentlemen, the worst thing is the reward which is being offered is not money but plutonium."

Kenny took up the conversation. "So we have our agents in the Middle East as well as Egypt trying to find out who may have their hands on plutonium, and who would have the wherewithal to pull off a stunt like this."

"Brock, how did you find out about the story of the diamonds? We assume that your roommate, O'Shea, might have offered you this tale. My guess is you didn't learn it on the farm in Indiana."

Before Kenny could continue, Admiral Higgins once again had a timely interruption.

"Son, if you haven't already surmised, we need to know two things. One, do the diamond exist, and two, if they do, where the hell are they. The United States doesn't give a damn about tale of diamonds, but when some crazy is out there offering to give away plutonium for them, well, that catches our interest."

"Sir I don't know," I nervously replied. "Tommy O'Shea did indeed tell me this story one night, and I, without his consent, decided to turn it into one of my research papers." I mumbled, "What a mistake that was.

"At the time Tommy had me believing that the diamonds were real, but I have my doubts now. Maybe this navy life has made me more cynical, I don't know. To address the second part of your question, the whereabouts of the diamonds, Tommy passed out before he got that far. I never really got a chance to ask him any further questions. I wrote the paper as is, and a few days later he found out and stormed out of my life. We haven't spoken since. The rest is history."

Admiral Higgins was now pacing around the room. I could tell that tension was very high.

Kenny spoke. "Admiral!"

"I know," replied Higgins. "Seaman Brock, Kenny wants to borrow you. He feels that even though it's a long shot, he wants you to go to Ireland to find your friend, O'Shea, and find out the truth about those damn diamonds and hopefully in the process catch the bad guys before they get their hands on them. And maybe if we are real lucky, we can find out who the hell is offering out plutonium from the Middle East."

"Sir, I'm not an agent; I'm a Seal."

Kenny interrupted, "We are not getting anywhere now with either U.S. or British agents either in Ireland or the Middle East. Or what I meant to say," stumbled Kenny, "is that it takes time to acquire information through normal channels and procedures, and, Seaman Brock, I don't think we have the time.

"Admiral Higgins has given us permission to use you or any United States naval asset that might help. We are counting on your inside acquaintance to help us with the two things we need to know: One, are the diamond real, and two, most importantly, where are they now."

"Sir, are those my orders?" I turned to Admiral Higgins.

"Yes, son they are. You are to help Agent Kenny and assist agents Smyth and Gibson until they determine you're no longer needed anymore. Then you can return to your Seal unit."

Higgins pulled out a cigar from inside his white naval jacket and started to light it. He stopped, looked me in the eye, and said, "Son, I know this sounds like a wild goose chase. We'll probably see you back here in a few days."

It was a new day and I found myself reminiscing. Austin Brock, international spy. Right! I was still reeling from my meeting yesterday with the staunch Admiral Higgins and his band of merry bureaucrats. My last orders from Higgins was to pack my things. I had eighteen hours to clear my activities with my superiors and get my butt to the air force base for a flight to Norfolk, then on to London for further briefings.

When the door of the large transport in Norfolk opened, the steps were already rolling up to meet the plane. The sun exposed a silhouette of a large man riding on the top of the stairs.

"Father Brock." A voice, followed by a huge hand, extended toward me. "My name is Jim King, CIA." He clutched my hand for a firm bone-crushing shake and then grabbed my duffel. "Come on. We don't have all day. You can call me Boomer!"

At the bottom of the steps was a black Suburban. Throwing my stuff inside, I jumped in, and Boomer and I were on our way. "I read about you. You're pretty much a green horn, other than that brief vacation in Kuwait," growled Boomer. "Oh well. At least they sent me a Seal to work with, so at least if we need to swim back across the Irish Sea, we'll be in good shape."

Boomer pulled the truck up in front of a guarded concrete-block building we walked in and were greeted by Kenny, still wearing the same suit he had on twenty eight hours earlier, only bearing more wrinkles.

"I take it that you and Jim King have already become acquainted," Kenny opined.

"Yeah, I guess, if you call ten minutes of verbal insults while riding in a government-issued black Suburban getting acquainted."

Boomer scratched his two-day-old facial stubble, then turned and walked over to a bar in the corner of the room, helping himself to a glass of ice water.

"Pay no attention to Boomer. He's not exactly Mr. Congeniality; however, he is one of our best agents. James

(Boomer) King was an offensive lineman from Penn State University, then a brief cup of coffee with the New Orleans Saints, then onto the marines, where we saved him fifteen years ago."

"Sixteen!" shouted Boomer from across the room. Boomer continued, "Thirty or forty pounds of diamonds? I have read your manuscript, Father Brock."

"Just call me Austin or Brock or the combo, but don't call me father."

I knew that when I said that I was only encouraging him more. He then knew he was getting under my skin.

"Whatever," said Boomer. "Do you really believe this crap?"

"Well, I did at one time. I'm not sure now, but I guess we will find out."

"Men, come sit down and we will get started," ordered Kenny. "Even though there has been a lot of chatter from the Middle East, there has still been nothing from Ireland. If this is true, it's the best-kept secret outside of Area 51 here in the good old USA." Kenny continued, "Our agents have been in Ireland for weeks, posing as tourists. They have been in pubs, visited castles and churches, but nothing.

"We also have agents in Syria, Iraq, and Iran, as well as Saudi Arabia where we first started hearing the noise requesting the stealing of the diamonds. We expect some radical Saudi oil king is behind this. We are in the process of trying to narrow down the candidates. As far as the offers from the recipients from Syria, Iraq, and Iran are concerned, we understand Saddam Hussein leads the pack in inquiries. We should have finished him off when we first had the chance," Kenny added "We are afraid there will be several groups all in a race to get to the diamonds first. By the way, we are also watching North Korea and China. We can't believe they aren't trying to get into the fun as well."

CHAPTER 15:

"Back to Ireland," said Kenny. "We have not exactly gotten permission to have our agents nosing around on what the Irish believe is a wild goose chase. In fact, gentlemen, it would start a national incident. So I need not say this mission is top secret. If for any reason your identity is blown or you are somehow arrested or whatever, the United States will deny any knowledge or involvement. Basically, gentlemen, you're on your own. Oh yeah, Brock, because you're in the United States Navy, we, the U.S., can't take the risk or the possible embarrassment of something going wrong, so we are not arming you. Sorry!

"Besides, you're only needed to find Tommy O'Shea. You do have his address, don't you, Austin?"

"Yes." I replied. "I have his parents' address. You know I haven't talked to him, so I don't know if he still lives at home."

"Well, you're to find him and try to find out if he knows anything else, hopefully where the diamonds are now, or if he can narrow it down to at least some general location. If this information was passed down from generation to generation, maybe there's a family member who can help us. Austin, you still need to be discrete. Unofficially you're just there on leave, for a short vacation. Officially you're only to gather information and report back to Boomer. He will be assisted by British special agent, Ivy Johnson. They will be posing as just another married couple on vacation in Europe.

"However, agents King and Johnson will be armed and will have the backup of other agents, both us and the Brits, which you don't need to be concerned with now.

"Okay, men, our first objective once the diamonds are located is to try to talk to the monks or whoever the owner of the diamonds is into temporarily relocating them to a more secure place until this all blows over, or at least letting us guard them. I think it's important they understand we are just as interested in maintaining their enigmatic secret as they are. We must have them believe us and trust us. And that's where hopefully your friend O'Shea can help us.

"Keep in mind the Irish are our good friends. They just don't believe us and they very much distrust the English; nevertheless, we have to perform this mission with the utmost respect for the Irish government, and more importantly, the respect of the Irish Catholic church, if these diamonds end up to be real and hidden in a church or a monastery."

"Well, that's great." I replied. "So let me get this straight. I'm supposed to become reacquainted with a man I previously betrayed, a man who probably hates me, become his friend again, lie to him again, and you need me to maintain our secrecy so not to indicate our objective. So basically I have to betray him again. Oh yeah, then you want him to help us find the diamonds on top of that. Piece of cake! Guys, I can hold my breath for over three minutes in ice water while placing a death charge to the underside of an enemy ship, or I can break into an enemy fortress undetected and, like a ninja, free hostages. I can snuff out the bad guys and be on my way all within minutes before anyone knows what happened, but what you are asking me to do is totally out of my league."

Across the table from where I was sitting, Kenny pushed his chair back, rose, leaned over, and placed his hands palms down on the table. He was now only six inches from my face. "Son, I don't believe you understand me. No one is asking you anything. We're telling you!"

Kenny, standing erect now, said, "Do you think the CIA usually recruits outsiders to do their work? Look at King over there; he hates this idea, and quite frankly, so do I. But this is coming down so fast that we have no other option. Thank God for modern computer databanks or we wouldn't have found you. Austin Brock, you, son, are our only quick option.

"We realize it's a long shot that your Tommy O'Shea knows anything more than you do or, for that matter, we know. But up until now, your paper is the only thing written, even in Europe, about the existence of diamonds."

The previously quiet Boomer blended in some of his thoughts. "From what I understand, only a select few members of the Irish Catholic church know about these diamonds, and they are sworn to secrecy. According to myth, Saint Patrick took great care when selecting a plan for passing along the stewardship of these gems. What am I saying?" Boomer hysterically announced. "I don't even believe this nonsense!"

"Gentlemen, you both will be leaving tomorrow, flying commercial. Austin, you will be leaving here from Dulles Airport. James you will be flying out of Logan International. This is so that if some unexplained incident would happen, it might take a little longer for the press to connect the dots. Austin, when you arrive in Dublin you will appear to be on your own vacation alone. We will be giving you a cell phone. You won't need to dial it. It will automatically call Boomer when you push any button. You are to make contact at least once a day. If it seems like someone is watching you, they probably are."

Boomer said, "Yeah, you better hope it's not the bad guys."

"This brings me to you, Boomer. You will be making connections with agents Smyth and Gibson, and meeting your pseudo-wife, field agent Johnson. They will be briefing you more, and you two—that is, Mr. and Mrs. King—will be on your way. Your mission is to stay in contact with Austin and report back to me. Our objective is, once the diamonds are located—I should say *if* the diamonds are located—then we will attempt to convince the owners that they and the diamonds are in possible danger and offer our assistance, or at least at that point we can talk them into turning the diamonds over to the local Irish authorities for protection. This obviously will be tricky. If this happens we must immediately disappear. Boomer, the Brits are working on an emergency bug-out plan. That is an overview of our first objective. Our second objective is to try to catch the bad guys. If we can remove the real diamonds from the scene and secure their safety, then maybe things can become fun. We can play a game of sit and wait. Hopefully we will be able to bag some terrorists.

Kenny concluded, "Men, time is not on our side. Good luck!"

CHAPTER 16:

Well, I was on my way, and I was actually pretty excited about seeing Tommy. I was also pretty nervous; I didn't know what kind of reception I would get.

The long plane trip afforded me the opportunity to reflect on both my experiences with Tommy in college and my new assignment to collect information for the CIA. I was going over in my mind how I would approach Tommy and what I would say.

Could all the wrong that I caused because of my poor judgment in college be corrected?

Is it possible that all this crap that happened was fate? If these diamonds really did exist, by writing about them back in college I unknowingly helped the CIA expose a plot years later to steal them. Well, hopefully Tommy would forgive me.

Kenny provided me with a copy of my report on Mary Magdalene, which somehow got a from the university, to refresh my memory. This started me thinking all over again,

Could this story be true, are the diamonds real, and are they actually a gift from our holy Lord? Or are they really just diamonds that were stolen from the Egyptian pharoahs?

Six hours into my flight, I dosed off, falling into a deep sleep, totally exhausted from all that had happened. I hadn't been that mentally tired since Buds.

I was awakened (at least that's what I thought) by a brilliant bright light. I was not on the plane anymore; I wasn't anywhere. There was no definition, no lines or angles.

Thinking back on this experience, I realized I was not nervous or afraid. The light was actually comforting to me. It was like I was in a large white room; however, because there were no visible walls, there really was no proof of that either.

Am I in heaven? I thought to myself.

"No," came a voice resonating through my thoughts. "It is not your time, my son. The place where you are is inside yourself."

Just then a silhouette of a tall man appeared before me. He had long silver hair with a silver beard and was wearing a white robe.

"My name is Abraham; I am the protector of the gift that you seek. I was the selected one who rolled the stone back from the tomb. I also delivered my master's gift to Mary, and then on Mary's ascension into heaven, I made certain that the gift was delivered to Patrick, where it remains today. Patrick has safely secured the gift until my master returns to earth to retrieve it.

"My son, these beautiful stones you seek are not from the minerals on Earth. The brilliance of the diamonds is merely the goodness and the light that potentially shines in the hearts of every man, woman, and child.. You see, as long as this goodness—love and kindness—exist here on Earth, the diamonds will remain brilliant. The beautiful stones will remain until my master returns to retrieve their light along with the light in the hearts his people and take them back to heaven.

"I know, Austin, your heart is true and your intentions are noble, but you need not worry. The diamonds are safe. Go home, son!"

While his command was still echoing, I was awakened by the jolt of the jet touching down on the runway.

I was now in Ireland.

CHAPTER 17:

It was the middle of the night when I arrived in Dublin, and by the small ponds of water on the tarmac, as viewed from my small aircraft window, it looked as if it had been raining for some time. For a brief moment I forgot about the dream I'd just had. *Wow!* I thought to myself. *What a startling revelation.* The papers that I was reading about the tears of Mary were still lying across my lap. Obviously that was the prevailing thing on my mind when I fell asleep, and thus caused my dream. That's what I told myself, anyway.

I admit I was a little nervous about this trip and I couldn't explain why. I had traveled several times to hostile countries and had been in some very precarious situations with my Navy Seal unit, so this assignment should have been like a walk in the park.

After collecting my bags and hailing a cab, I headed to my hotel. I decided to get some rest, even though I wasn't tired, and start out in the morning to find the O'Shea's castle.

Morning came and the rain was still pouring down. I finished my cup of coffee sitting on my covered balcony overlooking downtown Dublin. In my hand was Tommy's address, and lying on the table before me was a map of eastern Ireland. I had ordered a car, which was scheduled to be delivered to the hotel within the hour, and I would be on my way. My strategy, I decided, was not to phone ahead but simply show up at the O'Sheas.

The phone in the room rang; it was the front desk informing me of the arrival of my car. I collected a few items, including my cell phone and map, and went downstairs to make the transaction for my rental car. Exiting the hotel in the drizzle, I realized an umbrella would have been a good investment. My thoughts of being unprepared to fight the elements quickly left when my eyes caught a glimpse of the ride provided to me by the Dublin cut-rate auto-rental agency. *Not exactly what James Bond would be seen in,* I thought as I stared at the dented-up four-door green Renault.

I laid a paper beside me with directions toward the O'Shea castle that had I scribbled from the map earlier. I estimated this would get me heading in the general direction, north of the city. There I would simply have to commit the male cardinal sin, stop and ask directions.

Dublin was a city trapped in time. It had old architecture that was simple but beautiful with its own richness of warmth and coziness. While driving down O'Connell Street at 8:00 a.m., there was this normal rush-hour feel that perhaps any blue-collar city would radiate, but once I turned my car onto the back streets, there was a whole new ambiance. Humble shops of various needs greeted the visitors with an allure that invited them past their shingles and in their doors. Crossing Queen Maev Bridge, I noticed a barge most likely filled with barrels of Guinness heading to destinations unknown. This wasn't exactly the gondolas in Venice, but I found it just as charming.

The rain had stopped now and the sky was clearing. I had been driving for about thirty to forty minutes, and Dublin was now in my rearview mirror.

I was so mesmerized by the beauty of this May morning in Ireland that I found myself simply driving without even knowing for certain if I was heading in the right direction. The road kept getting narrower and narrower, and civilization was a distance behind me. My windows were rolled down in my makeshift car, allowing the warm spring breeze to blow my hair and tickle my nose with the sweet sent of honeysuckle. The view was incredible; whoever named this place the emerald island was right on. On both sides of the road were steep rolling green meadows of grass. Gusts of wind turned the meadows into seas of endless rolling green waves. In the far distance, jagged rocks broke the landscape, which gave way to mountains. Straight ahead and far to the distance, I saw a speck in the road. As I drove closer the speck became an old man on bike accompanied by a sheepdog running alongside.

"Tell me, sir, am I on the right road to the O'Sheas?" I had slowed to an almost complete stop to make my inquiry.

"Many a road is the right road to the O'Shea castle," responded the old man.

I stopped the car and got out. The weathered-skinned man showed me a large smile exposing one or two missing teeth.

"You're not from around here, I would suppose," quacked the wiry native.

"No, sir, I'm not…"

"And from the United states of America to boot. I thought at first you might be a damn Brit," the old man growled. "Yes, you are on the right road. You have been driving on the O'Shea property for four kilometers and this road, along with others, will get you to the front door if you wish. In fact, lad, if you like I'll take you there if you will allow my dog and I to ride in you car."

"It's a deal. If you can get your bike and dog in the back, you can jump in the front."

He did, and we drove on.

"Now I'm certain you're not a Brit. No Englishman would ever offer a ride to a lowly Irish sheep herder. McClain's my name, Calvin McClain. I'm employed by the O'Sheas and you're giving me a lift to work, lad."

Calvin was the O'Sheas' head sheep herder and had held that position for thirty-six years. His predecessor was Calvin's father, and before his father was his grandfather, and so on. Seven days a week Calvin would faithfully ride his bike, rain or shine, nine miles one way to work, except if the weather was too bad. Then he would bunk over in his special room upstairs in the main barn.

I was grateful to have Calvin accompanying me on the remainder of my journey. Even though I was only a few miles away, it would have taken me forever to find the castle on my own. There were several roads that ran into the main road. I would have surely taken a wrong turn.

It was an enjoyable short ride with Calvin, but our trip was over.

"I'll be stopping here, lad."

Calvin pointed toward a cobblestone barn and two smaller accompanying sheds about five hundred yards from the stone and wood fence that paralleled the road. That's where our car crept to a stop.

"Much obliged, my lad, for giving an old man and a dog a ride, but this is where we part for now."

Calvin, putting his hand on my shoulder, nodded facing straight ahead. "Your journey, my son, will end or start over the ridge. There you will find the O'Shea castle. I hope you will find what you're looking for." With that, Calvin gave me a wink, gathered his possessions, and walked away.

For a moment before I drove away, I watched Calvin manage his bike and dog along a narrow footpath toward the barn. I smiled thinking to myself, *How did he know I was looking for something? Maybe I just met my first leprechaun.*

CHAPTER 18:

I think the realism of finally coming face to face with Tommy hit me like a rock. How would he receive me? What would I say? Was I even doing the right thing by just showing up?

I had rehearsed several options of my initial greeting in my head over the last several days, but now my mind was a blank. My palms were sweating as I gripped the steering wheel and drove over the ridge. There it was, about a half a mile ahead and off the road about five or six hundred yards, perched atop a large hill that I would estimate to be one hundred feet above the elevation of the road.

What a majestic sight. I was not prepared for the eminences of this structure. As I drove up the cobblestone drive, I saw large oak trees that paralleled both sides of the lane. The trees were a good sixty feet in height, but still they did not hide the large gray monster that lay ahead. This castle was gothic but very beautiful too. Gray limestone blocks shooting straight up to meet the sky were separated only by an occasional window. These magnificent walls ran for a good way before breaking into another direction, creating another wing, and finally stopping at an adjoining tower, which shot farther into the sky. The grounds surrounding the castle were very well kept, with shrubbery neatly laid out underlining the lower windows and close-cropped ivy that crawled up the walls of the tower resembling a hand slipping on a glove. There were fountains flowing into reflecting pools and statues that seem to guard the estate like soldiers on watch.

I parked my car slightly out of sight behind the main circular fountain so not to expose its hideousness. It didn't exactly look right parking it next to the Bentley that sat in front of the main doorway.

I walked up to a large wooden door, rang the bell, and waited and waited. I started to turn away and then I heard the latch rattle, so I stopped and waited for the door to open. When it did I was confronted by a staunch man in a red jacket.

"May I help you?" inquired the man as he looked at me from top to bottom.

"Yes, sir. I'm looking for Tommy, Tommy O'Shea. I am an old friend from college."

As I said my request, the look on the gentleman's face was as uninviting as it could possibly be. I experienced the most uneasy and awkward feeling.

"Who is it, Keller?"

The soft voice of a female spoke from behind the man.

"Someone's inquiring about Tommy ma'am. Should I turn him away?"

Just then a hand pushed the door open wider, crowding the man slightly away from the center of the door. A female shape then filled the same space where the man had previously stood. The image of a perfect woman stood before me, her slender, petite frame accented ever so by soft feminine curves flowing from her shoulders, past her waist and hips. Long legs completed the ensemble of a perfectly proportioned female body. She had long auburn hair and beautiful dark blue eyes, the same blue eyes as Tommy—well almost. They were close enough, and I knew she had to be family.

These deep blue eyes were now staring at me, waiting for me to finally respond.

"May I help you?" she asked.

I extended my hand. "I'm Austin Brock." With that, this beautiful woman reached out and embraced me with a big hug.

"Austin, please come in. I'm Ashley O'Shea."

Pressing me away but still gripping my arm, Ms. O'Shea stared at me hard, as if she were trying to read my mind. We simultaneously backed through the door together, she still clenching my arm and staring.

"Keller, take Austin's bag and tell Mother we have a guest."

Ashley momentarily let go of me to shut the door.

"I apologize for just showing up without a warning. I was hoping to see Tommy. Is he here?"

Ashley, now looking at me with a puzzled expression, grabbed my arm again. "My God, Austin. You don't know, do you? I'm sorry. Tommy passed away six months ago; he was killed in an auto accident."

I was not prepared for this shock—cold-cocked by a blind punch, thrown by a bully called fate. Tommy was gone.

"I am so sorry, Ashley. I had no idea." Her blue eyes were welling up with tears as I moved closer, putting my arms around her. Immediately I felt a bonding of our souls. The emotion of grief consumed us, but sharing it somehow seemed to be beautiful gift.

"Come along," she said as she pulled me farther through the huge castle. "Tommy mentioned you often, Austin. You were very special to him. How happy he would be knowing you were here."

This comment made me feel a little better. It seemed as if she could sense the guilt I was feeling for the way things were left between Tommy and me.

"You're so kind, but our parting wasn't in the best of terms. I came here hoping to mend our relationship."

Ashley smiled and looked up as though she was looking into heaven and said, "You just did."

We continued walking through another large cathedral-shaped room. What a magnificent room it was. Tapestries hung from thirty-foot mahogany-paneled walls. A white marble floor covered one hundred yards or so from end to end. Several stained-glass windows depicting religious events added color and lightened our path.

"Are you hungry, Austin? Please join Mother and me. We were just about to sit down for some dinner."

"I would love to," I replied as she led me through a double door. On the other side an older, very dignified woman stood, a woman all off four feet tall. And there was those same blue eyes.

"Mother, this is Austin Brock. Do you remember Tommy talking about Austin?"

"Yes, of course I do. Come here, lad."

Tommy's mother gave me a bear hug around my waist. "We finally get to meet Indiana Austin. My name is Catherine, but you can call me Mother like the rest."

Mother was grinning from ear to ear.

"The rest of the family are in England on business—that is, my husband and the three boys still living at home. However, I know they would love to meet you if you can await their return in a couple of weeks. Honey, are you hungry? I'll bet you're weary from traveling. Keller is almost finished preparing dinner. Please sit."

Keller came out of the kitchen carrying my bag.

"Sir, your bag is ringing," he said as he handed over it to me.

"It must be my phone." *Oh shit,* I thought to myself. *I forgot to report in to Boomer.* "Hello!"

"Where the hell are you?"

"Hello, James. It's good to here from you too. I have just arrived at a friend's house. I'll have to call you back. Give a kiss to Ivy. Bye bye." With that short, abrupt response, I flipped my phone off and looked up across the table to two women staring back at me with their mouths open. Realizing how short I must have sounded on the phone, I felt compelled to respond. "I'm sorry, ladies. Just an old navy buddy. He always calls at the wrong time, and I can always talk to him, but conversing with two enchanting, beautiful ladies, well, that's something one doesn't get the chance to do that often."

Well, I think they bought it. They both shyly smiled and thanked me and we all three returned to eating a fine lunch prepared by Keller.

"Tell me, son," Katherine asked, "where and how long are you staying?"

"I am staying in a hotel on O'Connell Street in downtown Dublin, and as far as how long, I have not decided."

"Well then I will decide for you," said Katherine. "Well at least your lodging arrangements. You must stay with us. We have twelve guest rooms for you to choose from, and you can stay as long as you wish."

"Yes, Austin, you see you really don't have a choice. When my mother makes up her mind, there is nothing you can do." Ashley looked across the table with her pretty smile. "And besides, I know if Tommy were here he would also insist."

"Okay, girls. How could I say no to that, but my stay must start tomorrow. I need to finish some business in town tonight, but in the morning I'll return."

"Well, if that's the way it will be, then at least let us send Keller for you tomorrow. There is no need for you to rent an automobile when you're staying here."

"Yes, I can drive you anywhere you'd like," interjected Ashley. "In fact, that's what will do tomorrow. I'll show you the countryside."

"That sounds wonderful. By the way, I met your head sheep herder, Calvin. What a delightful man. I gave him a lift here after I stopped to ask for directions. He nearly talked my head off."

Both girls turned and looked at each other and laughed.

"So you've met Calvin, have you? Well that settles it, Austin. You must be a good man. We love Calvin; he's part of the family. The O'Sheas have employed the McClains for centuries. And it seems like Calvin has tended our sheep for one hundred years himself. The thing is with Calvin he rarely speaks to anyone unless spoken to first, including the rest of the help, or even the family. Even so, Calvin's always there for us when we need him. It's like he just appears; he's our guardian angel. I guess it's not exactly true that Calvin rarely speaks. He does spend a lot of time talking and visiting with the priests or the nuns who come calling from the local monastery. We worry about him riding his bike such a distance every day. We have often asked him to move in with us, but he always refuses.

"One of the mysteries about Calvin you may find interesting, Austin, is that legend has it Calvin is a direct descendent of, of all people, the great Saint Patrick. Well at least that's what our family has always claimed."

It was time for me to go, so after bidding my adieus I made my outside.

With a kiss on my cheek from Ashley, I crawled into the green Renault and drove away, only to slow momentarily and look when I passed by the sheep barns. I knew I'd better call Boomer back soon before he went berserk. So I grabbed the phone out of my bag and pushed the send button.

"Austin!"

CHAPTER 19:

"Sorry, Boomer. I couldn't talk earlier. I was at the O'Sheas', sitting across from Tommy's mother and sister. I have bad news. Tommy died six months ago in a car accident; I am not sure what to do next."

"Okay, Austin, we need to meet. There is a small café near your hotel. We will pick you up out front of your hotel in about three hours."

"That should give me enough time to get back. See you then."

The drive back was much different. My head was swimming and I couldn't stop thinking about Tommy. It was strange; all the events that took place today had given me no time to just stop and think. It was still hard to believe Tommy was gone. I had just lost my best friend, and the only thing I could think of was how I was now going to find the tears or Mary.

Like clockwork, a car pulled up in front of the hotel three hours later. I opened the back door and crawled in.

"What's up, Seal boy?"

"Too much, Boomer." I was staring at the back of a the neck of a woman sitting next to Boomer on the driver's side. "So this must be your new wife." I leaned forward to make my formal greeting.

"This new wife is not happily married. I'm Agent Ivy Johnson." She turned to me and winked. "And I'm on the toughest assignment of my career, pretending to be this Neanderthal's better half."

"Ha-ha, limy bitch," Boomer muttered under his breath.

British agent Johnson was a tall brunette with a very proper, almost frumpy, British demeanor; she was very neat and organized—the polar opposite of Boomer. It was easy to tell who the brains of that outfit was.

We found our café and went inside. The place was empty, except for the help. The hostess led us to a back room, where agent Kenny and British agent Smyth were already sitting at a table, drinking Irish coffee.

"Gentlemen and lady, please have a seat." Kenny greeted us then thanked the hostess and shut the door behind her as she exited the room. "Austin, I'm sorry to hear the news about your friend Tommy. But we have to move on and move on fast. Boomer, did you sweep this room for bugs earlier?"

"Yes, sir. I also checked out the owners of this establishment. It's all clean here."

"This seems like déjà vu. Every meeting, we are gathered behind a large table like some happy family, right Boomer?"

"Whatever, boss."

"Whatever indeed." stated Ivy.

Kenny set down his cup of coffee and stood up.

"We do not have the luxury of time; yesterday we received information of break-ins of two churches, one near Clare and St. Michan's church here in Dublin. The reports from the local papers indicate minor vandalism and nothing turned up missing. The police do not think there is any connection. Because this being somewhat of a covert operation, we are not privy to any police reports. We believe that the diamonds were not found. Otherwise there would be a lot of chatter. These morons can't keep their mouths shut. This may be the only thing on our side. We are afraid violence will probably occur if they don't get what they came for soon.

"King, you and Johnson need to continue touring churches, monasteries, and whatever as tourists. Be a little more aggressive with your questioning of the priests and monks. Mr. Brock, I need you to hang out with the O'Sheas. See what you can find out. Other family members must know what Tommy knew. Keep in contact, share information. Agent Smyth, what do you have?"

"British Intelligence thinks they have a lead on which Saudi oil baron is behind this. Back in the mid-1980s, it was thought that a significant amount of plutonium was smuggled out of the former USSR and sold on the black market. We have always suspected the purchaser to be someone from the Middle East and had narrowed it to a short list. As far as whom we think the henchmen are, we suspect two groups, one group being from North Korea. The other group were sent by our good friend Saddam Hussein. The CIA has agents in Saudi Arabia and they are prepared to take out this oil king. And, Austin, your Seals are there to retrieve this plutonium, just as soon as we have our target. That's all I have for now, sir."

"Thank you, Smyth; we will update via meetings whenever needed. Good luck people."

We adjourned our meeting and Boomer and Ivy drove me back to my hotel. I was ready to retire for the evening.

CHAPTER 20:

After grabbing a quick bite to eat, I was ready for some major sleep. What I wasn't ready for was a visitor. I fell asleep quickly and was awakened by a bright light illuminating the entire room. I had seen this light before. This was the same brilliant light that had accompanied Abraham and had visited me in my dreams on the plane. Was I dreaming again? I rose in bed, seeing a silhouette by the door moving toward me. "Abraham, is that you?"

"Yes, my son, and no, you are not dreaming. My good son, your quest for the diamonds is noble, but because you did not heed my warning and return back to your home, you will be put in great danger. Many evil ones are also searching for the gift which does not belong to them, but the diamonds will always be safe from those whose hearts are impure. If you insist on your pursuit, find sanctuary with the one who tends the sheep."

"I must have fallen back to sleep, or maybe, I never really woke up, I don't know. But this time I was awaked by the maid knocking on my door, wanting to clean my room. I had overslept. I had made arrangements for Keller to pick me up at nine and it was already eight thirty. I still needed to return the Renault and check out of the hotel. The maid was still knocking at the door. Maybe she couldn't hear me rustling around.

"I'll be right there!" Still in my boxers and nothing more, I got out of bed and walked across the room to the door. I was expecting to see the maid when I opened the door. Instead my heart stood still.

"Ashley!"

"Good morning, sunshine."

This radiant beauty stood there staring and smiling at me in my vulnerable situation, acting like the cat that just ate the canary.

"Ashley, what are you doing here?"

"I couldn't wait for Keller to bring you to me, so I decided to go fetch you myself."

Her eyes moved down my body and were now staring at my almost exposed lower half. Her face turned as red as her lipstick.

"Maybe you should get dressed," she whispered.

"Ashley! What a surprise. I thought you were the maid.

"So do you always greet the maid in your underwear, Austin?"

"No, I've been having weird dreams lately, causing me to oversleep, and I guess I wasn't thinking when I opened the door."

"So you couldn't wait to see me, huh?"

We laughed and exchanged a hug and kiss.

"Give me a few minutes to shower, shave, and pack and I'm all yours."

I was quick to gather myself, minding what my father had always taught me: never keep a women waitin, especially a women like this.

"All I have to do is get rid of that ugly green car and we can be on our way."

Ashley replied, "Don't worry about the car. My father owns the rental company. We'll just leave the keys in it. I'll call Keller and he will handle all the arrangements for its return."

So away we went. I thought to myself, *If only my friends from back home in Indiana could see me now, being chauffeured around Ireland by a beautiful woman in a Bentley.*

Ashley smiled and said, "Today I thought I would show you around Dublin and maybe some of the countryside if we have time. Most of all, I just thought we could talk. I would very much like to find out more about you, the United States of America, Indiana, the things you and Tommy did at school, et cetera, et cetera. Maybe you can even tell me about your dreams that you've been having."

"As much as I can't wait for you to show me around, I look more forward to us finding out all there is to know about each other. In fact, I don't intend on leaving Ireland until we both do."

The day was wonderful, and Ashley was a great tour guide. We drove some; we parked and walked some, I was finding out everything about her childhood and she was finding out everything about mine, with a tidbit thrown in here and there about the landmarks and history of Dublin. The problem was I was so engrossed with her I forgot what I was supposed to be doing (asking her about the tears of Mary). It was about one o'clock and we were getting hungry. Ashley selected a favorite pub of hers in the Dublin market area. The pub was located next to a flower shop displaying its wares on the street; I took advantage of the opportunity and bought her a bouquet of yellow carnations, which in turn won me a kiss. We grabbed a table on the sidewalk out front and ordered two Irish coffees with Jameson's whiskey in memory of Tommy, whom we saluted over and over for every round we ordered.

I don't know how long we were there, but I know that we were both getting smashed and our conversation was becoming more and more open.

"Ashley," I said as I took both of her hands and looked her into her eyes.

"Oh my God. You're not proposing to me already, are you? But if you are, the answer is yes. Ashley Brock. That has quite a ring to it, don't you think, my dear?"

"Stop joking around. I'm trying to talk to you about something important."

"I am sorry, my love."

She was now pulling herself closer to me, practically climbing on top of me. The glow of the candle on the table illuminated her face, which was now only inches from mine. She was not making this easy.

CHAPTER 21:

"Ashley, did Tommy ever tell you what happened between us?"

"Is that's what's bothering you, Austin? Yes, he did, but not at first. We could tell someone hurt him very much. I guess that everyone expected it was a girl; in fact, even today I'm the only one in the family who knows that it was you that hurt him. Tommy and I were very close. We were the closest in age. I always thought we were on the same wavelength. Well, I knew it wasn't a girl that broke his heart. Anytime someone would inquire about you, I could tell he was lying in his response. It's strange, but I think he was trying to protect you. I was alone with him at the horse stables several weeks after he came home and I finally confronted him. He told me what happened; he told me he told you about the tears of Mary and how you used the story for a school report, or something like that, without his permission."

"You must have hated me for hurting your brother. Maybe you still do." I was too ashamed to look at her in the eyes as I spoke.

She took her hand and placed it under my chin, forcing me to look her in the eye; I prepared myself for what she might say next.

"Austin, you are just like him. I had no feelings at the time one way or the other about you. My response to him was I started laughing. Boy that pissed him off. I said, 'Tommy, you mean to tell me that all this is about is that tale that our grandfather used to tell us, sitting around the fireplace after he had just drunk one or two pints of whisky?' I continued, 'By the way, Tommy, did you ever wonder why the story was always changing just a little depending on how much he had to drink? I can't believe you are willing to throw your friendship away over this.' You know, Austin, Tommy wouldn't speak to me for two weeks. Finally he came up to me one morning and gave a hug from behind and said, "You know, sissy, you're right once again. I've been a fool. Austin did not know he was betraying me and I was not man enough to forgive him.'

"So there you go, Austin. Tommy forgave you, and in fact he was probably as guilt-ridden as you for the way he had acted."

"So why didn't he answer the letters I sent?"

"You know, I don't know why. I never knew about the letters until after his passing. However, I know Tommy wouldn't have saved them if they didn't mean something to him. Maybe he was too embarrassed or ashamed; I guess we we'll never know."

"Austin, I found your letters and read them. You really touched me. I want to thank you for loving my brother the same way my family did."

What would you say, Ashley, if I told you that your family's little tale may possibly be true? Well, at least some oil king in Saudi Arabia believes that the diamonds exist, to the extent that he has put an offer out for them in plutonium to trade for the diamonds. This, as you may have guessed, has drawn a crowd of really bad guys in a quest for this treasure. Ashley, I have told you about me being a U.S. Navy Seal, and you obviously know about my infamous college report of the tears of Mary. Well, so do the United States and England now. Apparently my school papers interested the CIA, especially after they intercepted intelligence concerning this plot to recover the diamonds. Obviously it's not stealing the diamonds that concerns the free world; it's the plutonium winding up in the wrong hands."

I immediately could tell this conversation was turning Ashley cold. She took the bottle of whiskey and downed the last swallow without any dilution of coffee; I knew I had struck a nerve.

"So let me get this straight, Austin. You came over here to Ireland not to patch up a friendship with my dear brother, but instead you wanted to use him again for your selfish gain. You really are a bastard. Damn you, Austin Brock. This story the tears of Mary may not mean as much to you and I, but to Tommy it was more than just a story. It was carrying on Irish tradition; it was the love of his ancestors and the internal belief in all that is good. He shared something very personal with you, something he strongly believed in, not just some mystical story of Irish folklore. Tommy shared his heart and soul with you and you betrayed him, not once but twice."

Ashley, with tears running down her cheek, stood up from the table and fell against it just enough to knock over the accumulated cups, glasses, plates, and a chair. She staggered quickly across the room and ran through the door.

"Ashley, wait!" I pleaded.

I threw some currency on the table and chased after her. As my feet hit the sidewalk, I saw the door to the Bentley slam. It was parked about a block away on this now darkened and disserted market street of Dublin.

Knowing she had no business driving in her condition, I ran as fast as I could try to stop her. I was not able to, but the light pole at the edge of the curb did the job. I arrived just in time to put my hand on the door handle, but I couldn't release the latch. She jumped the sidewalk and hit the light squarely, sending it crashing to the ground.

I pulled open the door. Ashley's head was slumped over the steering wheel and she was crying. I examined her and asked if she was injured. She did not verbally respond, but she appeared to be okay. I slid her over to the passenger seat and crawled in. The car survived the incident almost unscathed; however, the light pole looked to be totaled. I knew the best thing was to get the hell out of Dodge. Explaining this to the Dublin police did not seem to be in our best interest at this time. Taking care of this situation looked like a job for Keller first thing tomorrow morning. So I drove us back to the castle. It was late and we both had had too much to drink.

For a day that started out so wonderful, it sure ended up lousy. I thought after our day together she wouldn't have reacted the way she did. I was now hoping it was just the whiskey not her rational thought.

The ride home was quiet; Ashley was passed out, her head pressed against the passenger window, which was now fogged up with her breath. I was a little nervous about my ability to find my way back to the castle in the dark, being that I only was there once and that trip was made during the daylight hours. However, I made it. When I turned the car down the long lane leading to the castle, I was relieved, even though it was late and I wasn't looking forward to Katherine O'Shea's reaction as I carried her drunken daughter over the threshold and up the steps to her bedroom. At least we were back and not in the Dublin city lock-up. When I pulled the car up to its normal parking spot directly in front of large entrance doors, I noticed no lights were on. Trying to wake Ashley was futile. I thought over my dilemma and my options. It was late and apparently everyone was asleep. Ashley was not waking up. She had the key, I assumed, in her purse. I had no idea where her room was or where I was to stay, so I thought, *What would a seal do?* There were two options. The first one I immediately rejected. "I am not breaking in," I muttered out loud. The second option was to wait it out, which seemed to be the most appealing. I turned off the engine and reclined our seats as much as possible. I unbuckled Ashley's safety belt and covered her with her sweater, and we were camping there until the morning.

"Wake up, wake up, Austin!"

I was awakened by an excited female voice and a pounding on my chest, waking from my sleep to the morning light and Ashley practically on top of me.

"We need to go inside. I have got to pee, and then I need to throw up."

The car door flew open, and she darted toward the door, fumbling for her key along the way, which as it turned out she didn't need. As she arrived at the door, it swung open with the help of Keller.

"Good morning, Miss Ashley," Keller greeted her as she bolted past him without a response. I could tell by the smirk on his face that he knew she was not feeling up to a nice chit-chat.

"Good morning to you, Mr. Brock. I hope you're feeling somewhat better than the young lady O'Shea. If I may retrieve your bags from the car, you can follow me to your room. By the way, lad, I wouldn't mention to Lady Katherine of your sleeping in the Bentley or of how you managed the small dent in the front grill."

"Thanks, Keller. By the way, there is a broken lamp post with Ashley's name on it in the market area of Dublin, and a rental car needing to be returned at the hotel. Ashley said you—"

"Not to worry. I'll take care of it," replied Keller.

"I can get my bags. Thanks anyway, Keller," I responded as I clutched the handles to the suitcases and pulled them out of the trunk, closing it with my shoulder. I proceeded to follow Keller into the house, stopping momentarily to glance at the distant view of the sheep barn before entering.

"Something interests you from across the meadow, son?" Keller inquired as he shut the big door behind me.

"Well, I was hoping to catch Mr. McClain sometime; I enjoyed our brief conversation and would like to visit with him some more while I was staying here."

"Good luck, lad; he's a mysterious one, that Calvin McClain. People go down to the barn to see him and never catch him in, but somehow the sheep always get fed and the wool is always sheered and bundled, ready for market."

Keller turned to me and chuckled.

"I have been employed here for over twenty-five years and I have never been able to run into Calvin on my own terms. You don't find him; he finds you."

I followed Keller up a long spiraling set of marble stairs, then down a seemingly endless hallway before reaching my room.

"Here you are, lad; I hope this meets all your requirements. "

Keller opened the door, exposing a beautiful room. It was quite modern. It even had a television.

Just as I was about to receive my tour of the room, my cell phone began to ring.

"I will leave you time to settle in. Someone will retrieve you in an hour or so for breakfast." With that, Keller pulled my bedroom door shut, leaving me to myself.

CHAPTER 22:

Ring! Ring!

"Hello, Boomer."

"Things are not good. Have you seen the news, Austin?"

"No, what's up?"

"We are in Clare, the site of a recent church break-in. This morning two bodies were discovered face down in a field, shot in the back of their heads, execution style. That was part one of the news, part two is that they were two North Korean men, with expired visas. Agent Kenny believes that they were snuffed out by their competition. Lucky for us there are now fewer bad guys to worry with."

As you can imagine, this place is now crawling with local police and reporters. Agent Johnson and I are bugging out. Our friends who did this are probably on to the next church in the next town anyway. We are pretty sure that they whoever they are, are touring all the churches where Saint Patrick either started or may have visited, hoping to find the diamonds, so that's what we'll do too. Hopefully we will get lucky and catch these bastards soon."

"Anything on your end, Austin?"

"No not really. You two be careful. I'll talk to you tomorrow." I stuck the phone back in my pocket and surveyed my room on my own.

CHAPTER 23:

My room was about as large as the rest of the castle, but surprisingly it seemed very cozy. I went about the task of unpacking and started the shower to warm it; thankfully this guest room had that luxury. I wanted to recharge my batteries and then after breakfast try to see Calvin. After laying out my shaving kit on the adjacent sink, I slipped out of my clothes and entered through the glass partition doors, feeling the hot water hit my chest and the icy cold exertion as my feet met the cold granite tiles of the stall. This exhilarating experience did have an immediate charge; it reminded me of my first hot shower back on board the aircraft carrier after our mission in the gulf war.

After about ten minutes or so and halfway through rinsing the shampoo completely out of my hair, I thought I heard a noise from my room.

"Is someone there?" The echoes I created came bellowing out like bad feedback from a rock concert, but my shouting was met with no responding voice, so I discounted the noise and continued rinsing my hair to complete my shower. I turned off the valve, shutting off the water, and reached through glass door to retrieve my towel, but it wasn't in the spot where I left it. Confused by this circumstance, I slid the door open wide to reveal the mystery. There sitting on the marble vanity, holding my towel in all her smugness, was Ashley.

"Feeling better?"

This flip comment was all I could think of on a moments notice, and after all, I was completely naked and dripping wet. She tossed me the towel and gave me a sheepish smile.

"Well, our last bedroom meeting I was deprived of seeing you fully nude, so I thought I would try again. "If first you don't succeed then try again. Isn't that the fundamental motto you American's live by?"

She seductively slid off the vanity and approached me (now at my full attention). She slid her hands through my wet hair. Then clutching the back of my neck, she pulled my face to hers. We kissed for what seemed to be an eternity of sensuous bliss. Just as she had me at my most vulnerable point, she broke free, pushing me back while taking in my naked body. With one quick glance she exhaled a sigh of seductive breath.

"Seeing you, Austin, in the buff was worth the wait. The anticipation of our making love must be even more beautiful. Our time will come."

She left me standing naked, wet, and now in total frustration. I stepped back into the shower, closed the door, and started up the shower, this time turning the water to cold. As the water hit my face, the door opened and a hand came in and shut the water off.

"Oh yeah, my love, I forgot. I was sent here to retrieve you for breakfast. Keller wants to know how you like your eggs."

Pushing her back, I closed the door and started up the shower.

"Scrambled!"

Well, if there was any question if Ashley was still mad I guess the answer was no. *Now I wonder if she even remembers last night at all. I know one thing. I have become deeply attached to her in a short period of time, and I think she has become deeply attached to me as well.*

I found my way to the dining room to find Katherine and Ashley waiting patiently. Covered plates and empty cups with saucers awaited my arrival. Keller was sitting in a chair in the corner, reading the paper, and peered over the print when I entered the room.

"Top of the morning to ya, Master Brock."

"Top of the morning to you, Katherine. I'm sorry I'm late. Please forgive my rudeness. I didn't realize that you were waiting on me."

"When there is perpetuity, there's no burden caused by deferment,"; Katherine graciously greeted me.

"Except when one's deferment causes others' eggs to cool." my interjection drew a laugh from the girls and even made Keller smile.

After a delightful breakfast, Ashley escorted me to the library.

"Austin I had a most lovely time yesterday but I want to apologize for it's conclusion. I had way too much to drink, which led to me overreacting. My emotions are churning inside of me. Since Tommy's death it seams like any little thing sets me off."

"Well, a pint of whiskey is not exactly a little thing. I must say I was a little apprehensive about my coming here to see Tommy and telling him I was on a mission to recover the tears of Mary. In fact, I expected him to react the same way you did, whiskey or no whiskey. However, I was confident that after I explained the circumstances behind my mission he would totally support me—hopefully maybe even help me track down the diamonds before the bad guys got their hands on them. I really thought that all this was some sort of fate and that as a result it would mend our friendship."

"Well, I believe in fate as well. I know Tommy would have helped you if he could. Maybe his baby sister might be the next best thing, and I would love to help."

"I have found you some books on Saint Patrick here in our library, along with maps of his travels. If Saint Patrick hid the diamonds, maybe this might shed some light, or maybe some clues where he might have hidden them. Also I might try and get in touch with my father in London. He's not expected home for a few more weeks; however, with some persuasion he might be of some help, although he would probably think you were crazy."

"Thanks, Ashley, for your help. Yes, I believe that your father would think I was crazy too and would probably order me out of your house immediately. This whole thing is a little hard to explain over the phone. The books may be of some help; however, both U.S. and British Intelligence have been pouring over books and religious documents for weeks, coming up with nothing."

"Do you have any family diaries, dating back to the early centuries?"

"Yes, Austin, we do. I don't know why I didn't think of that. Most of the top shelf is filled with diaries, except the really old ones, which are kept in a specially humidified glass case to protect the pages. This glass case is in my father's study. I will take you there."

"Yes, but first, Ashley, take me to visit Calvin. You said several things that intrigued me about him, mainly the fact that Saint Patrick was an ancestor."

CHAPTER 24:

Ashley and I walked down the cobblestone drive toward the sheep barn. The aroma of honeysuckle accented the morning air as well as the sounds of pebbles cracking under our shoes as they surrendered their size to our weight and the larger cobbles, which they became sandwiched between. The only other sound that rivaled this came from the chirping of the birds.

Ashley took this time to tell me of her memories as a child, walking down this lane to see the newborn lambs or just to visit with Calvin if he was in.

"Austin, I have not seen Calvin since the morning we received word of Tommy's passing. In fact, he came up to the house right before the phone call and ended up spending the day praying and consoling us. Once again Calvin's there when we need him. I guess that's what shepherds do—tend their flock."

We entered through the fieldstone gate and walked the remaining steps leading to the huge barn. When we arrived I was taken aback by the magnificent architectural beauty of this structure; this was no barn that I was used to in Indiana. The three-story fieldstone structure had stained-glass windows and brass lion head latches to the doors and shutters. This building looked more like a cathedral than a barn.

"Well go on in," ordered Ashley.

I turned the latch and opened the door, exposing a dark cavernous room. She reached around me, flipping a switch, turning on the lights to a room that had the appearance of a stateroom of a wooden ship. As we entered through the doorframe, the smell of damp wool and wood smoke quickly made reference to this place being a place of work, not worship, as its facade would have suggested.

"I do not think he is in," I surmised. Ashley opened up a large double door on the opposite side of the room.

"Calvin are you here?" she shouted through the opened doors. "It's Ashley."

"Come here, Austin; look out there."

I walked across the room and peered through the open doors down a flight of steps and into a more traditional barn-style room of rows of stalls filled with sheep. This room was immense but immaculately kept. It opened up to the elements so the sheep could come and go as they pleased. Across the way, two boys were cleaning out stalls, shoveling manure into carts, very much reminding me of my childhood days. The boys paused for a moment to respond to Ashley's shouts inquiring the whereabouts of Calvin; they shook their heads, acknowledging the unknown.

Ashley pulled both doors to a close, turned, and looked up the staircase that paralleled the adjoining wall.

"Up there is Calvin's office. I got a spanking from my father when I was eight for playing in there without Calvin's permission, and I haven't been in there since."

So we climbed the stairs. I could tell Ashley was apprehensive about returning to the scene of the crime for which she was punished sixteen years ago. Her actions, I thought, were cute. She still had the innocence of a little girl.

Ashley knocked on the door, we stood there for a moment, and then she turned to descend back down the steps.

"Wait a moment, Ash." I stepped around her and grabbed the doorknob. "I think it's open."

"Don't Austin!"

The door creaked. As it slowly swung open, a faint phantom breeze greeted us, puffing our hair. The room was empty of any human presence; however, it was exceptionally quaint. The room was naturally light because of stained-glass windows, which gave off an amber glow as the rays of sun beamed through. *Quaint* was perhaps not the best adjective that could have described the room. There was almost a reverent feel—the feeling of pureness—like that of a sanctuary of a church. The room's physical appearance was clean and orderly. A wooden table minus chairs centered the room. Placed on the table were a candle and what appeared to be a sterling communion set, which was illuminated by the beams of light from the window. Two of the four walls were bookshelves. The third was basically barren with the exception of what looked to be an old sea captain's trunk stowed in the corner. The forth wall was basically all stained-glass window.

"Let's go, Austin."

With Ashley's wish, I closed the door and we headed down the steps. When we reached the bottom, it occurred to me, "The window! Ashley, one of the stained windowpanes was a pot filled with what looked to be diamonds. I pivoted and ran back up the stairs. This time when I clutched the knob to open the door, it was locked.

"I don't believe it. The door is locked. How can that be?" I rattled the knob, but to no avail. I ran down the steps past Ashley and through the door. She quickly followed me to the side of the barn. Staring up in disbelief, I saw that there it was—an etched rendering of a pot and it was spilling over with diamonds.

Before we could catch our breath, Ashley nudged my arm. When I looked down at her, she was looking away from the barn. I turned to see what grabbed her attention. There he was, about thirty meters or one hundred feet away, leaning on a wood rail fence with a honeysuckle vine dangling from his mouth, just watching us as though we were there just for his amusement.

"Top of the morning, young lad and lassie."

We sheepishly (pardon the pun) walked over to Calvin. He was awaiting us, smiling from ear to ear. Ashley leaned over and kissed him on his cheek, which made him jump up and do a little Irish jig. We both laughed. It was the funniest sight. I could tell she was very special to him.

"How's my wee little pumpkin seed? You never come a callin' on old Calvin anymore. It's not cause you're too big for your britches now, are ya?"

"I'm sorry. Calvin. It's just that I haven't felt much like chatting the last few months."

"Oh, I miss the days when you used to come down to the barn and hide from your brothers. We had a grand time, now didn't we, dearie."

"Calvin, do you remember Austin?"

"Oh, yes. How can I forget a man with a kind heart giving a ride to an old man and his dog."

"So I don't suppose you two peas in a pod are just here to admire the barn's windows, now are ya?"

"No, Calvin. I mean, I still love just visiting with you, but Austin and I need to talk to you about something."

"I know, I know, you want to know about Mary's diamonds. I see it in your eyes."

"Ashley, remember the picnics that we used to go on? We would talk for hours. Do ya suppose we could have a picnic just like old times—you, me, and our new friend from America? I do my best talking after I've munched on one of those tiny sandwiches Keller makes."

"Well that sounds lovely, Calvin."

"Yippee," cried the little Irishman as he clicked his heals and trotted away, with a parting instruction for Ashley: "I'll meet you at Murphy's rock in one hour."

We looked at each other and smiled. Ashley commented, "Once again we didn't find Calvin. Calvin found us."

"Come on, Austin. Let's go get a picnic put together."

"How far away is this Murphy's rock?" I asked as we left the confines of O'Shea castle, Ashley clinging to a blanket and I clutching a well-prepared basket full of sandwiches, fruit, and buttermilk, Ashley and Calvin's traditional spread for this occasion.

"It's a fair hike, mostly vertical; however, the view is well worth the effort."

CHAPTER 25:

The hike was fantastic. Even though our trek was a little rugged at times for Ashley, I could tell she had made this trip hundreds of times when she was younger. The excitement on her face was priceless; it was as if she was a little girl again.

We finally made our destination a little over an hour from the time when we departed and left Calvin back at the barn. However, I didn't think he minded our tardiness. When we arrived, Calvin was sitting on this huge rock. I surmised it to be Murphy's rock. His back was to us, legs crossed. Beside him sat his dog. He could have been praying or just taking in the ambiance. I can't imagine him or anyone ever tiring of this breathtaking view.

"Calvin, we're here," announced Ashley, thinking he had not heard our arrival.

"Yes, dear. I know, and twenty-two minutes late. One thing about we Irish is our punctuality, something you should learn, my lassie."

Calvin jumped down from the rock and gave Ashley a tweak on her nose with his finger, then directed us to follow him to a patch of clover, where we spread out the blanket and made camp. The three of us ate our lunch and Ashley and Calvin chatted about times past, both happy and sad. When it was apparent that Calvin was finished with his meal, I started the conversation that was our main objective.

"Calvin, I'm here as a friend, but also I'm here on a mission from my government. The United States along with the UK believe some terrorist organizations may be after the diamonds called the tears of Mary, and we are concerned not only for the sanctity of the diamonds but the safety of those who are the guardian of them. I know of the great secrecy behind this, and the need for this secrecy; however, it's not secret anymore, at least to some very bad people who are here now in the country and are very aggressively searching for this secret, the diamonds. We used to be concerned whether the diamonds were real or just a myth; however, it really doesn't mater now. The risk of danger is still the same. The bad guys believe the diamonds are real; therefore, they will do anything to obtain them. They have already killed once trying to find them, and I'm sure they will do it again.

"My question to you, sir, is, assuming the diamonds are real, do you know where they are and would you help us retrieve them before someone evil does?"

"My son, you're a good lad with admirable aspirations; however, your faith is week, as is unfortunately the faith of many others. An old friend of mine, Abraham, has visited you twice. Did not Abraham ease your mind as to the safekeeping of Mary's sacred treasure? Do you honestly think that heaven would allow any unworthy individual to acquire this treasure, let alone someone evil like those you mention? Believe me, the tears of Mary are very safe and secure, and divulging their location to you will only cause you great strife."

"It is not about finding the diamonds. Calvin; it is about finding bad people looking for the diamonds. I have a sense of duty to my country as well as a personal duty to myself, my beliefs. When I was on a mission with my special forces over in Kuwait, I wasn't just fighting an aggressor trying to take over a country. I felt in my heart I was fighting evil—an evil more dangerous than any one man or army. I feel that same feeling now. This is a race against evil. This burning feeling in my heart will not go away until I have done everything in my power to help subdue these people, these terrorists, this evil."

Calvin walked over to me, put his hand on my shoulder, and looked deep into my eyes.

"My son, the war against evil has been around since the beginning of time and will be around until our savior returns to drive his mighty sword into the belly of Lucifer himself. There are noble people such as you all over this world, just as there are evil people all over the world. No one country lays claim to the monopoly over either.

"If you wish to find these evil men, follow the path traveled by my dear cousin Patrick, from Saul to Dublin. This obvious route seems to be their strategy. Fools!"

Calvin released his grip on my shoulder and walked away, training his focus on his dog. I turned to Ashley and said, "Did he just say his cousin Patrick? Not his ancestor."

We both turned our attention back to Calvin, but he was gone. Ashley called out," Calvin!" and then after a few moments, "Calvin!"

"Ah, I hate when he does that. He's gone, Austin, I guess our picnic is over."

"Ashley, sometime we've got to talk about that guy. Suddenly I believe in leprechauns, and not the one running along the sidelines at South Bend, Indiana."

"Well let's head back to the library. We can look through those old diaries; maybe we can find some additional information. I need also to call my colleagues to update them and to receive additional instructions."

So we packed up and headed back to the castle.

CHAPTER 26:

"That's funny, no one answers. This government-issue cell, slash satellite phone only calls one other phone; it's my only link to my superiors."

"So maybe they're out."

"The CIA is never out, Ash! They have been here in Ireland as long as I have and are already doing what Calvin suggested, following the path of St. Patrick. They were only a step behind the two Koreans shot in their heads a couple of days ago."

As we arrived within site of the castle, I noticed a different car parked in the drive.

"It looks like you have company, Ashley."

"I don't recognize the car," she said with some concern in her voice.

I grabbed Ashley's hand and we picked up our walking pace until we reached the front door. She stepped in front and opened the door. We rushed in to find Katherine and Agent Johnson conversing on the settee in the entry hall.

"Cousin Austin, so wonderful to see you, I've finally tracked you down."

Agent Johnson jumped up and nervously gave me a peck on the cheek, and a weak hug.

"I didn't know you had relatives in Europe, Austin."

"I didn't think I should mention it. The fact she's English and all. You might have thought differently of me."

There was an uncomfortable moment of silence while everyone stared at me in my most awkwardness. Then thinking of nothing else, I began to laugh until, one by one, everyone joined in.

"You probably want to catch up with your cousin. Come on, Mother, let's get some tea." Ashley hooked her mother's arm and escorted her from the room, looking back at me, very puzzled.

"Austin, hand me your phone," Agent Johnson said.

I quickly pulled it out of my pocket and handed it to her. She diligently pried open the back of the unit and with a few snips from her manicure scissors, she rendered the phone useless.

"The mission is aborted. I have new orders to deliver to you before I return to England."

"Where is Boomer?"

"He's being detained by the Irish authorities in Dublin and questioned regarding the two North Korean chaps found executed in Clare. Obviously, Austin, you haven't read the papers the last few days. Don't worry about Boomer; it's only a matter of time before they release him as well. You see they also questioned me but had nothing to detain me on. Their hang-up seems to be that we were recognized by locals nosing around the same church before and after the crime, and because we both have temporary visas, well, it looks suspicious.

"Because of the potential political embarrassment, our governments feel there is too much at risk. All our special agents have orders to immediately leave Ireland. This mission moves to plan B."

"What's plan B?"

"I'm afraid you are. You're plan B. Right now you are pretty much on your own. Kenny says your orders are simple: Just find the diamonds. Here is a new phone. Call only when you must. Otherwise, wait for Kenny to contact you. Oh yes, one more thing. I have orders to give you this." Agent Johnson pulled out a 9mm automatic and handed it to me. "There is something else, Austin. The phone."

"Yes. the phone. I suppose there was a reason you destroyed it?"

Johnson hesitated. "It's our phone. We seem to have misplaced our phone. When the police came to our hotel room, Boomer quickly hid the phone under the mattress. Original, huh? What a dumb lug. That's the first place anyone would look. However, the police didn't search our room before they took us to their station. If they did they would have probably found the special phone, along with our guns, which I quickly hid in the toilet tank. When I returned to the room later, after my interrogation, the maids had already tidied our room. The guns were there but the phone wasn't. I questioned the hotel staff. They denied seeing the phone but did state they found the room in shambles. When we left, the room was fine. I believe someone searched our room while we were gone. Maybe it was the police; maybe someone else.

"Austin, that phone was not just a phone. It was a listening devise. We could hear all your conversations. This was something Kenny insisted on. CIA policy. For the last two days while the phone was out of our hands, anything you've said potentially someone else has heard. Rest at ease your new phone doesn't have that nifty feature.

"Well, I must go now. Good luck, Austin."

As a parting gift, special agent Johnson kissed me on the cheek, then whisk herself from the room and out the door.

"Your cousin looks nothing like you, Austin, and apparently she is not one for long visits, now is she."

I slid the gun down my pants and spun around to see Ashley standing in the hall, holding a tray loaded with a pot of tea and accessories.

"She's not my cousin, but I have a feeling you know that, don't you."

"Sorry, I couldn't help but hear most of the conversation. It was all I could do to keep Mother away. She is nosier than I. By the way, pretty unprofessional of a British Intelligence agent not to check first to make sure that no one else was listening before divulging secret information. Well, anyway, what's next?"

"Let's head back to the library. We need to retrace St. Patrick's journeys according to Calvin, so in order for that to happen, we need to study."

CHAPTER 27:

I grabbed my maps of Ireland from my room and met Ashley in the library. She had already selected a couple of books and had them open and displayed on the large mahogany table. Ashley was up on a ladder, still searching diligently for that one book.

"Ah, here it is!"

She pulled out and dusted off what appeared to be an old Irish school text, entitled simply *Saint Patrick*. She began scanning the pages before completely descending from the ladder. When finally finding what she was looking for, she began to read out loud.

"Saint Patrick journeyed from Wales via a small sailboat, passing through the treacherous Narrows of Lambay Island, past the mountains of Mouine, to the waters of Stangeford Lough on to the mouth of the Slaney River, finally taking land at Slane.

"So, my love, that's where we start. Slane."

"Actually that's where I start, Ashley. You're not going. It's way too dangerous. The men I am hunting for play for keeps. They're armed terrorists who have little regard for human life. Basically they are cold-blooded animals with very distorted ideals, ideals fueled by some crazed evil tyrant. I can't take a risk something might happen to you."

"I appreciate your chivalry, sweetheart, but you need me. You need an automobile and someone who knows Ireland real well. And I can provide you with both. I have been to every square inch of this emerald island. You can cover a lot more ground not having to read maps and stoping for directions. Oh, I forgot. You American gents don't ask directions, do ya?"

Ashley stood up from her side of the table, walked around behind my chair, and leaned down, sliding her arms under mine and around my waist. I could feel her breath on my neck as she began seductively kissing my neck and cheek.

"Austin, don't be worried about my safety. I can shoot that gun you have stuffed down your trousers as well as anyone and better than most, maybe even you."

She reached down and placed her hand around the grip of the pistol, as if to indicate to me that I wasn't hiding anything from her.

"Be careful. It might go off," I whispered in her ear.

"The gun or you?" she playfully responded. "Oh come on, Austin. Please let me go. I will be a valuable cohort, and believe me, the moment any danger occurs, I'm gone."

"Well, against my better judgment you can go. You are right. You can certainly help me navigate the country faster and maybe I will appear less conspicuous traveling with an Irish mate."

"Hey, I like that. Traveling as your mate. Maybe to be less conspicuous I could be your wife, Mrs. Austin Brock. Has a ring to it."

"All right. Play time is over, miss." I stood up from my chair with Ashley still attached to my back. Only now she wrapped her legs around my waist and constricted her grip.

"Hey, American sailor boy, I don't think you're so tough. What's that you're called again, a sea lion?"

Ashley quickly turned from sexy seductress to a playful giggling young girl once she got her way. It was apparent with her, as is with most beautiful women, that she had mastered her skills of femininity to impose her will on you without you even having a clue what she was doing until it was too late.

"That's Navy Seal, you Irish brat," I growled teasingly as I flipped her over my shoulders and onto the table, where she lay flat on her back.

Our faces were now only inches apart. The smile on my face slowly faded as my eyes were drawn into Ashley's. Caught by the moment I had immediately fallen into a hypnotic trance of passion. Unfortunately that mood was about to change.

"Showing Ashley some crude American customs such as table-top wrestling, Master Austin?"

Simultaneously we both looked up from what I'm sure looked like a most ridiculous position, at least from Keller's vantage point. He was entering the room, carrying a paper under his arm and holding a pot of coffee.

"Oh, I see you already have a pot of tea. Well, anyway here is today's news. I'm afraid not much about the good old USA. Mostly articles covering the rash of break-ins to religious landmarks around the country as well as the execution of those two Korean lads. Police now believe both of the men murdered have ties to terrorist organizations. Also the article goes on to say that they have released the American ex-football player with a lack of evidence connecting him to the crime."

Keller set the paper and coffee pot down beside us as we climbed down from our provisional stage, trying to be as dignified as conditions would permit.

"Well here you are anyway. If there is nothing further, Miss O'Shea, I will retreat back to the kitchen and allow you two to carry on, to read the paper or return to wrestling, whatever your desire."

"Read the paper," I said as I laughed and mimicked to Ashley Keller's instructions while watching him leave the room. "Why bother, he pretty much told us all I need to know already."

"I'll go pack and tell Mother we are leaving for a few days to tour the countryside."

I acknowledged her with a nod as I continued on reading, cramming as much information as possible about Patrick's travels and the churches he started. It quickly appeared St. Patrick had basically covered every square kilometer of Ireland. If one would be looking for the treasure of diamonds, it would be like looking for a needle in a haystack. I looked up for a moment to see the newspaper laying in front of me; it quickly occurred to me these guys were leaving a trail a blind man could follow. All I needed to do was figure out where they had been and overlap that information with St Patrick's landmark, find out the places they hadn't been yet and go there and just wait. It also occurred to me that it was only a matter of time before these bungling marauders would be caught by the local authorities. With all this publicity being churned up by the media and every local and national police force looking for these bad guys, plus the heightened security to all churches, cathedrals, and landmarks, our nosing around has just become more difficult.

I turned my reading now toward the newspaper to see if there was any theory given as to why these break-ins were occurring. The consensus given was that it was still a mystery. *That's good,* I thought to myself. There was no mention of diamonds, terrorists, oil barons, Iraq, etc. If that theory somehow got out, it would create mass hysteria, and God forbid, the secret of the tears of Mary would be no secret anymore. All the religious landmark would be ravaged and destroyed by greedy fortune hunters.

Ashley returned to the library to find I was still enthralled in my reading.

"You're still here!"

"I'm having Keller, prepare a car for us. The Bentley has a date with the auto repair garage tomorrow, so I requested the Jaguar. That's my fathers favorite car. I'm sure he won't mind our using it while he's away."

"I assume that he has never seen you at the wheel, especially after leaving a pub with several pints under your belt."

"Very funny, Austin. You need to go pack so we can get on our way."

"Ashley, according to my earlier reports, the churches that were broken into were two churches in Clare and St. Michan's church in Dublin. The paper adds two more to the list just recently, St. Doolaght's church near Portmarnoch and yesterday St. Patrick's Cathedral. Same story. Nothing seems to be taken, just overturned tables, bookshelves, broken vases, etcetera. Well I think we can eliminate these places from our itinerary. I don't expect they will make their return at least in the near future.

"All right, Ash. I will run to my room and pack a quick bag. Please gather up this stuff. You can read on the way while I drive."

Fifteen minutes later I returned with my bag in hand and united back with Ashley, who was waiting at the front door. Katherine arrived at the same time as me, carrying a paper sack.

"I have packed a few corn muffins and persimmon jelly for your trip."

"Austin, do you expect to rendezvous with your cousin on your journey?"

I looked at Ashley, then back at Katherine.

"I rather doubt it ma'am. She was going one way and we are going the other."

Katherine nodded. I could tell she wasn't completely on board with my answer; however, she immediately turned her attention to her daughter.

"Ashley, do you have your cellular phone on you?"

"Yes, Mother, and I will be sure that I call once we have arrived this evening. I promise."

"And you will stay in nice familiar bed and breakfasts which we have stayed in the past?"

"Yes, I promise, Mother, and please don't tell Daddy when he calls. He'll only worry. He is worse than you about that. Mother, I'm twenty-four. We'll be fine."

Ashley gave Katherine a kiss, and we proceeded through the door to an awaiting XKE and a smiling butler.

"Madam O'Shea, Master Brock, your carriage awaits you."

We all were quite amused with Keller's humor. He acted as if he was sending us on our honeymoon. Well at least three of the four in attendance were amused, but I don't think Katherine appreciated his wit.

The concerned look in Katherine's eyes as our car pulled away had me second guessing my decision to let Ashley accompany me on this journey. Katherine had no idea what we were heading off for, but still she was worried. I could not imagine the pain she must have endured losing Tommy, and I knew that her mother's intuition was bothering her now as she saw her only daughter ride away with a guy she barely knew.

Worried mother or not, we were on our way. I was committed to my mission and now committed to the total safety of Ashley.

We were off to Slane, for no other reason other than it was believed to be the first landfall of Saint Patrick after returning to Ireland. According to my quick research, Patrick was born in Kilpatrick, Scotland but was kidnapped by Druids and taken to Ireland as a slave to tend sheep. Turning from his loneliness and despair, Patrick became close to God, sometimes praying for hours straight. He remained enslaved until he was twenty, when God came to him in a dream, telling him to escape via the sea. So he found some sailors who took him back to Scotland, where he reunited with his family. Some years later, after becoming a priest, Patrick had another dream, only this time he was told to return to Ireland to save the people from the Druids and to convert the pagans.

Next to me sat my beautiful navigator giving me verbal directions to get us underway while at the same time perusing the books she had selected to help us with our research.

"Sweetheart, I was a young girl the last time we visited Slane village; however, I do remember exploring the Slane castle with my brothers. I remember it had an eerie, gothic feeling, but I don't recall many details other than that. The castle was nearly destroyed by a huge fire a few years ago and I think it hasn't reopened yet to the public. I don't believe that Saint Patrick had any real involvement with it or its original owners anyway."

Ashley didn't speak again for two hours, other than giving the occasional direction or two, her nose buried deep in her books.

We finally took a break when I stopped for gas and got out to stretch our legs.

"Austin, the Hill of Slane is where we need to go!" Ashley shouted as I jumped out of the car. Before I could respond she was standing beside me, holding the book up to my face. "The Hill of Slane. St. Patrick lit his first paschal fire at Easter in the year 433, announcing the arrival of Christianity in Ireland. Near the top also sits the ruins of Friary Church, built in 1512. This might be our place."

"You're right, Ash; that could be our place. At least that's a good place for us to start looking. Nice work, dear." Acknowledging her help, I gave her a slap on the bottom. Proud of her contribution, she flit away, turning her head around once to give me a smile. Again the little girl side of her came to the forefront.

After a soda to wash down Katherine's corn muffins, both the Jag and we were refueled enough to continue our journey up the coast.

CHAPTER 28:

"So where are we staying, girl, when we get to Slane?"

"There is a quaint bed and breakfast which is owned by my second cousin. Mother was supposed to call ahead announcing our arrival. This place is very romantic; the scenery is breathtaking. I will request a room overlooking the Boyne River. Very nice for couples honeymooning. "

She winked and punched me in the arm. Her nonchalant attitude was somewhat worrisome to me; it was a little too carefree for what might lie ahead of us. I don't think she really understood the real danger involved.

In the Seals it was constantly beaten into our brains that it was imperative to completely understand our enemies and never under estimate their capabilities. It was very important to never lose focus, or the consequences might result in either the loss of a teammate or your own life.

Slane village looked like it was carved into a steep hillside by Neptune himself. What an enchanting old Irish coastal town.

Our car rolled up to the cross street. On all four corners stood identical three-story limestone houses. It was probably a sight that hadn't changed for hundreds of years. We found out later these houses were built by four spinster sisters who wanted to keep an eye on each other's comings and goings.

"Drive straight through and up the hill a little farther. Cousin Bryan's place is on the right side," directed Ashley.

I pulled into the drive and we both got out. I grabbed the bags and followed her hesitant steps through the arched stone entrance gate and up the walk to the front door.

"So how long has it been since the last time you saw your cousin?"

She turned and gave me a nervous grin, and when her mouth opened to speak, the door opened.

There standing before us in the door was a dingy yellow undershirt stretched to the brink of tearing by a huge belly. Behind this behemoth belly was its master, a short, toothless, greasy-haired middle-aged man.

"Cousin Ashley," the belly spoke. This was obviously Bryan. He extended his arms wide and lunged toward a surprised— almost shocked—Ashley, giving her a bear hug.

"How nice to see you again, Bryan." Ashley's voice was muffled by the embrace of her newly reunited relative. She initiated her escape by slipping under his arms, freeing herself from his uncomfortably long greeting.

Bryan was obviously very happy to see his cousin and was very gracious to me as well; however, I was able to avoid his hug.

After his initial greeting, Bryan's Irish brogue made him virtually impossible for me to understand; even Ash was struggling at times.

Ashley's childhood memories of Bryan were totally damaged by the reality that socked her in the face today, and as for myself I was now just hoping we had clean sheets on our beds.

The adjectives that Ashley used in describing this bed and breakfast—*quaint, romantic,* and *breathtaking*—were all kind of stretch. Oh believe me, I been around a lot worse. Some of the inns I saw during my mission in Kuwait made this place look like the Ritz Carleton. Actually our room appeared to be clean, and although the windows were smallish, you really could see the Boyne River, and if you tried you could see the ruins of Slane Castle in the distance.

Bryan helped carry our bags to the rooms, then showed us the kitchen and the community bathroom at the end of the hall. He stayed to chat with Ashley awhile before excusing himself to attend to his chores. Our honeymoon wasn't exactly starting off well; Katherine had ordered us separate rooms. Oh well. I expected nothing less.

Ring! Ring!

Ashley came and sat down beside me on my saggy bed and watched me answer my recently acquired cell phone.

"This is Brock."

"Yes, I figured as much. This is Kenny. We show you are in Slane."

"What do you mean you show that I am in Slane?"

"Apparently agent Johnson failed to explain your phone to you completely."

"Oh you mean like you when you issued me my first phone and forgot to explain the listening device. Hey, Kenny, I thought we were on the same side.

"I understand that I owe you an apology. Our mission was seriously compromised by misjudgments and I will take the blame for that; however, our objective is still intact, and this mission is still on course."

"If you haven't already heard, Boomer was released from Irish authorities but was asked to leave the country and so he has. Boomer is with me. We are about ten miles out in the Irish Sea on a pleasure yacht cruising the coast line.

"Austin, your new phone is equipped with a global satellite tracking device. We now realize we don't need to listen to your every word; however, we do need to know your every location. If you need to talk with us, just hit any key, same as before, but if you can't talk and you require our immediate assistance, hit the nine key three consecutive times. This will signal us to engage to your location, and we will be there within minutes."

"What makes you think I need any of your help? If I can't take out this small group of shit heads on my own, I might of as well quit the Navy Seals and join the girl scouts."

"I know, cowboy. You're perfectly capable killing the bad guys on your own, but you need us to clean up the mess. Cluttering up Ireland with dead bodies will only land you in jail and charged with murder, and the United States will be totally powerless to get you out. Do you think anyone will believe you're whacked-out story about saving diamonds from terrorists?

"Austin, you're smarter than that. When things get hot, you call us. We will come and dispose of the bodies and sanitize the scene. Then we'll all bug out. Understand?"

"I understand, boss."

"I have no additional information for you at this time; our intelligence chatter gave us nothing relevant. Your choice of checking out Slane is good, but if it looks like a dead end, move on. Well if there is nothing else, Austin, we will sign off."

"Asshole!"

I hit the off button and tossed the phone in my open bag laying on the floor.

"Do you believe that guy. He understands he owes me an apology! Oh yes, and apparently agent Johnson failed to explain my phone to me."

During my conversation with Kenny and my subsequent rant I forgot I was not alone. I turned to find Ashley quietly staring at the floor.

"I'm sorry. Have you ever had a disagreement with your boss, wow!"

I was hoping that this poor attempt at humor would break the ice. Obviously something she heard from our conversation was bothering her. She still did not move from her trance.

CHAPTER 29:

"Honey, what's wrong?"

I put one arm around her and with my other hand I combed back her hair with my fingers as to better see her eyes, which were now focusing sadly into mine.

"So when you're done with your mission, you're just going to bug out. I'm not really sure what that means, but it sounds like you are just planning to leave abruptly, and if I'm at the scene, are your friends going to sanitize me as well? I guess that I wasn't prepared for this to end so quickly. I was hoping to be more than just a temporary part of your plans."

I laughed softly and gave her a gentle kiss on the forehead.

"Well first off, those bastards are not my friends. They are only counterparts. And secondly, there is no way in hell that I am leaving Ireland without you, and thirdly, if anyone's going to sanitize you, it's going to be me. Where is the soap?"

With that I pretended to wash her with my hands, then wildly messing up her long hair as if I was shampooing it. This started her giggling uncontrollably, which led to her biting my arm to get me to stop. The next thing I knew we were entwined, rolling around on the bed, uncontrollably laughing, until our laughs became silenced by frantic kisses of passion.

It was at this moment I realized that I was falling in love—in love with an Irish beauty, my late best friend's baby sister.

I could tell she was already in love with me by the way she gazed into my eyes, a stare that went straight through to my heart. This impassioned, piercing look from her ocean-blue eyes I had seen twice before. The first time was when we were sharing pints of whiskey at the corner pub in Dublin, and again most recently I saw it when we were wrestling on top of the table in library.

We couldn't tear off each others clothes fast enough. We were two lust-driven white-hot half-naked bodies, wet with passion and dripping perspiration, waiting to explode.

We were auling each other's bodies, playing out some unquenchable ritual of foreplay, when out over the end of Ashley's feet and the protruding bed posts I spied three pint-sized children about four or five years in age standing at attention, sporting big smiles on their, faces waiting patently for us to notice them.

"Children!" I shouted, and Ashley screamed as we both jumped out of bed, Ashley ripping the sheet off the bed in one quick motion, covering her exposed body. I myself stood there in my boxers looking perplexed as one of these little pixies raised her arm to show us a fistful of fresh wildflowers they had apparently picked as a gift to give to us.

"Ah, aren't you darlings precious," declared Ashley.

Ashley responded warmly to the children, taking their bouquet and giving them each a kiss on the tops of their little heads.

Enamored by the charm of these three cute kids, Ashley became caught up in the moment, sitting on the edge of the bed, talking to them for several minutes before they scampered away.

"Aren't the local children so adorable?"

"Yes, very adorable indeed, and yet they have also reminded us the need to always lock our doors."

By this point I was dressed and almost finished unpacking. Talk about killing the mood. I had just experienced what most married couples with young children must contend with at times, a lack of privacy at the worst possible moment.

"Oh well, I guess our time will come," Ashley said as she smiled and blew me a kiss while slipping her jeans on from across the room.

"I think your mother called ahead and ordered these kids sent to my room at the most opportune time as some sort of chastity deterrent."

"Cool off, Romeo, while I go unpack, then we can get something to eat and turn in to our own rooms for some sleep. My guess is you want to get an early start in the morning and just as well, we not make love tonight. I might tire you too much. I need you at your top level if you need to fend off the bad guys tomorrow."

"Right, tire me out. Whatever. We'll see who tires who out, baby." I retaliated by throwing a shoe, hitting her in the ass as she bolted out the door.

Well, for that night Ashley pretty much had predicted the future. We did exactly what she had said. We ate supper with Bryan and two other couples in the dinning room, then I walked Ashley to her room, gave her a long goodnight kiss (which she said would have to last me), and retired to my room for the remainder of the night.

CHAPTER 30:

I was awaked by the wind blowing rain against the window pane like pellets from a BB gun. It took me a moment to realize where I was, anywhere but the bed provided me by this bed and breakfast. I was instead on the floor in the middle of this room, lying on my back, staring at a crack in the ceiling. I knew my partner in the other room was still fast asleep, so I took this opportunity to get in my ten-mile run, rain or no rain.

The aroma of freshly ground coffee filled the air as I walked down the narrow stairs and out the front door, trying to be as stealthy as possible as not to alert anyone, especially Bryan, of my departure. Carrying on a conversation with Ashley's cousin without her alongside to act as interpreter was an option I was not prepared to undertake.

The rain pellets that had been spraying my window earlier were now stinging my face as I ran up the narrow street toward my recently chosen destination (the top of the Hill of Slane). It was a hard run because of the steep grade and the loose cobbles in the path, which played havoc with my footing; however, the rain did eventually stop and the pure beauty of this location came out, making the challenge worth the reward.

About halfway up I focused on a tower in the distance; upon my arrival I realized it was part of the remains of the Friary Church. The remaining structures looked the same as I envisioned from the description that Ashley gave me from the book she was reading yesterday.

Slowing my run down now to a fast walk, I approached the tower, and after a quick survey I entered. Cautiously unhooking the latch, I swung open the small wooden door, which gave a long screeching sound that announced my arrival. A narrow flight of sixty-two steps led me to the room at the top, where I was immediately astonished by the panoramic view of the countryside. Directly below I viewed a graveyard with an unusual looking gable-shaped tomb as its centerpiece.

The rain had long since stopped and now the morning sun was creating steam. It was like a fog bank rising up from the ground. The black birds I had been watching picking in the soil around the gravestones were now totally shrouded under the wall of steam.

Suddenly, breaking the silence of this serene morning was the screech of the wooden door sixty-two steps below me. My first thought was it must have been the caretaker or maybe a tourist, so I decided not to startle my new guest. I would announce my presence.

"Hello!" I called out, but a few seconds passed and there was no reply. "Hello!" I raised my voice further and stuck my head into the doorway.

Thud, thud! The wood frame of the door next to my head exploded. Someone was shooting at me. I quickly spun around and fell back against the wall, reaching under my T-shirt and down the back of my pants, grabbing my nine-millimeter, advancing a round into the chamber to return the favor. Then I spun myself back in front of the door and squeezed off two shots down into the darkness. I heard the sound of the door slam, so I ran over to the edge directly above the door and leaned over the side to see a vague profile running away through the fog. My shot was not clean, so I decided to give chase.

Down the steps I flew, crashing through the door as if were made of paper. When my feet hit the dirt, I was at full speed.

Where was that bastard, I thought to myself, running while keeping my head on a swivel. At ground level, the steamy fog bank did not seem as bad; however, I had not been able to catch up to the shooter.

I sprinted all the way back to the street, seeing nothing but goats and geese. Frustrated, I stuck the gun back in my pants and headed back to the house.

About one hundred meters or so from Bryan's house, I spotted a figure running through the gate and up the steps. I couldn't make out the face from my distance, but I did recognize the figure.

"Ashley!" the echoes bounced off the cobblestones and rolled down the street, orchestrating a perfect volume and clarity, but this caused no reaction from her. I could see the door open and close, letting her enter the dwelling.

I made my way, a few minutes behind her, traveling through the gate and up the steps and on into the house. Bryan was busy vacuuming the rug in the front room; his back was toward me and he didn't hear me enter, so I darted up the steps and down the hall past my room. I was standing in front of Ashley's door. I started to knock, then hesitated a moment. I decided to take a step forward just to stand close to the door to listen.

Why didn't Ashley stop when I shouted? Where was she coming from? She didn't mention she was a runner, too.

All these thoughts were racing through my mind. Maybe it was paranoia. My experience is that getting shot at does that to you.

I reached my hand out and gripped the doorknob. It wasn't locked so I twisted it and pushed my head slowly through. On the floor were discarded articles of clothing as if she was in a big hurry. Something wasn't right; I continued on in and closed the door behind me.

'Ashley, are you here? I walked across the room, leaned into the closet, and turned on the light. It was obvious she wasn't here unless she was under the bed, and yes, I did check there as well. I leaned over and picked up the T-shirt laying on the floor; it was moist with sweat. I then raised it to my nose. I took a whiff. I was relieved only to smell the lingering sweet fragrance of her

French perfume, and not the unmistakable stench of gunpowder, a telltale sign of when someone fires a handgun.

Somewhat relieved, I went back into the hallway, thinking to myself, *She must be in the bathroom at the end of the hall.* And sure enough, the door was shut.

My discomfort returned when I stuck my key in the lock of my own door. I noticed that it was not completely shut. I once again pulled my pistol out of my pants and pushed the door the rest of the way open with my foot. I entered the room with my gun fully extended.

The room was a mess; however, nothing was taken. I had left nothing in the room of value. My identification and passport, as well as my wallet and my gun, were on my person.

Was the thief in my room the same person who shot at me in the tower? Did he or she have an accomplice, or were both incidences just coincidence?

I know one thing: Whoever he or she was who shot at me, they were fast. Even though they had at least fifty meters on me, I still thought with my speed that I would be able to catch up before we reached the bottom. Hell, I wasn't even able to see them let alone catch them.

What a slob!

Ashley entered my room daunting me only in a towel and with her hair done up in a turban wrap. She was obviously referring to the mess and assumed I was the culprit.

I was about to start my interrogation of her when I noticed in her hand a small radio with wired earpieces. I then looked into her eyes. She immediately sensed my frustration.

"You didn't do this. did you?"

Ashley's voice took on a concerned tone. By this time I had exonerated her in my mind of any wrongdoing. Maybe she was a good actress, but my heart told me to trust her despite my brain telling me not to trust anyone.

"I have had quite the morning. I'll explain to you while I help you pack. Things here just got a little to dangerous. I saw you running earlier. I yelled but you didn't respond."

She looked down at her handheld radio and said, "I can't run without my music. Sorry, sweetheart."

"Well that explains you ignoring me; you had me worried for a moment."

I grabbed her arm and led her back to her room.

"Austin, what happened? Why are we packing? Where are we going?"

Ashley rattled off these questions while she quickly dressed, watching me plop her suitcase on the bed and begin shoveling her clothes into it.

"In the order of your questions, first off, I was shot at while on my run this morning, and when I returned back here I found my room broken into. Secondly, this place is not secure enough. That's why we are packing. Thirdly, I am sending you home. Someone this morning tried to kill me but only missed by a couple of inches. If you had been running with me instead of by yourself, you might have caught that bullet instead of the doorframe. I told you when things got too dangerous I was sending you home. Well, they are and I am."

Ashley didn't argue. She was noticeably shaken by what had happened. Her fantasy, the excitement of chasing after a treasure of diamonds, and the possibility of danger became a serious reality of life or death. I was also awakened by this reality and ashamed that I let my selfish emotions toward Ashley cloud my better judgment. Letting her go with me in the first place was a needless risk and I wasn't about to keep on endangering her life.

Ashley was ready to return home, even though she didn't want to leave me. I could tell she was extremely torn, but she knew that I was a professional and that I would be better off completing my mission not having to worry about her safety.

Before I put her in her car to send her on her way, I had her help me ask Bryan several question, including if he saw anyone nosing around the house or if anyone else was staying here besides us. Bryan's answer to both questions was no.

I also needed a car, so she inquired for me if there was anywhere I could rent something. Obviously there wasn't, but Bryan, the good soul that he was, offered me his vehicle, and I had no other choice but to accept his offer.

I knew that Ashley needed to tell Bryan and later her mom something about our abrupt change of plans, but she couldn't tell them the truth. So I told her to tell them that she couldn't give them any specific details and that they couldn't tell anyone, but that I was U.S. special agent working with the Irish government and that I was chasing down some bad guys. I figured that this would work with Bryan but Katherine would never buy it.

I told Ashley to tell Bryan that someone might be watching us, so I wanted it to appear we were both leaving Slane. When we were a mile or so out of town she would let me out and I would hike back and he could check me into another room. If someone was following us, I would be able to catch them.

Bryan did buy our story. In fact, he seemed almost giddy about being able to help in any way. I'm sure this was major excitement for him or for that matter anyone from this small, quaint village, where watching the grass turn green in the spring was usually all the excitement these people got. Hey, I know all about small-town life. It doesn't mater what country it's in.

I carried Ashley's bags to the car and looked the car over very well, including underneath. If someone was trying to kill me, a car bomb would be a viable option. We were, in fact, in Ireland.

Ashley gave Bryan a hug and a peck on the cheek and then got into the car; I also gave him a convincing handshake as to appear to anyone who may be watching that I was leaving as well, hoping to entice them to follow so I could make my capture.

Ashley was driving while I kept a close watch for anyone who might be following. Unfortunately it appeared no one was. There weren't a lot of vehicles in Slane, Ireland, so it wasn't hard see if we were being tailed or not. As we began to drive, I found myself staring as much at Ashley as I was looking at the road behind.

Slane disappeared from view about two miles out, so I had her pull over to the side. She had both hands on the wheel, staring straight ahead.

"I love you, Austin. You had better return for me soon, or I will be back to look for you."

She slowly let go of the wheel and turned to me. Tears were streaming down her face. She began trembling as I gently took her in my arms, and we fell into a long passionate kiss.

"As soon as I take care of this business I will be back to get you. Please don't worry. These guys are pussy cats compared to what I have been used to fighting." I grabbed my bag and got out of the car. Standing in the middle of the road, I watched the Jag speed away till it finally disappeared in the horizon.

CHAPTER 31:

I bypassed Bryan's place and went directly back up Slane Mountain. I needed to get back there as soon as possible. Maybe I interrupted something earlier and quite possibly the shooter could still be up there. I also wanted to keep a low profile by returning to Bryan's after the sun went down. This would only help with my anonymity.

I did spend the rest of the day on Slane Mountain, revisiting the Friary Church tower, then on up to the summit. This time I was not alone. I was joined by several tourist, young and old. The crowds being what they were, I knew that this was not the ideal situation for the diamond thieves to find their booty. Nor did I expect to find them with signs around their necks, announcing there intent. So I decided to hang back and observe, profiling the people. I was looking for one or two individuals of Middle Eastern or Asian descent. What these individuals would be doing I had no idea.

I would anticipate perhaps they would return after dark, carrying hammers or picks, maybe shovels, to do their excavations or unearthing.

Well if that might be their plan, so it must be mine as well, I thought.

I left the mountain at sunset and returned to an ever so gracious Bryan, who had assumed his new self-appointed roll as my special protégé. The language barrier was great between Bryan and me and without Ashley there to be my interpreter, it was a struggle. However, Bryan did understand this and did his best with visual aids. He had laid out old copies of extremely worn spy magazines along with the James Bond book *Gold Finger*. While showing me these, Bryan would pat me on the chest with his hand, then pat his own chest, attempting to signify his knowledge of such matters, at the same time trying to obtain a bond with me.

I just nodded my head and smiled.

Under the moonlight and with my night-vision goggles I again trekked back up the mountain and staked out until dawn. Once in position, I called Kenny, filling him in on what had happened and my planned strategy. Keller updated me on intelligence and informed me that they were on alert, awaiting my signal to respond, and could have agents there in twenty minutes or less.

Unfortunately my night came and went and with no visitors, at least the kind that walked upright and packed automatic weapons and sported excavating tools.

For the next three nights I staked out the mountain, and with the same results, nothing!

Maybe it was time for me to leave; maybe whoever tried to kill me four days ago was long gone.

The boys on the boat were becoming just as antsy as I; constantly calling me on the satellite phone. Boomer was even calling just to chat. He told me that he took a break in between throwing up to see if he could switch me places. He is pretty much a land lubber and has been constantly seasick since he got on the boat. The truth is right now I would switch places with that pathetic lug in a heartbeat.

CHAPTER 32:

Ashley was tapping her tea cup with her spoon and staring into space while Katherine read the morning paper.

Somber was the mood this rainy morning. The girls were brooding over missing their men. Keller had just returned from driving James, Katherine's husband, to the airport. James was heading back to London to join his sons and complete their long and arduous business dealings.

Katherine was happy when he or the boys came home for a few days, but it seemed it was weighing harder on her more and more each time when they left.

Then there was Ashley; she was a mess, stewing around the last two days in her pajamas, not even going outside for her routine run or walk. (She usually did one or the other religiously.)

It really didn't much matter if the girls were conversing or not, they were both in their own little worlds and wouldn't really listen to what the other would say regardless. In fact, Keller would walk through the kitchen, passing several times by the table where the girls were brooding, basically being unnoticed by either female.

Ashley did, however, faithfully tell Katherine Austin's edited story per his wishes. And as he had predicted, Katherine had her doubts as to its validity. However, she didn't push the issue, Katherine knew her daughter was in love and she could tell Ashley was not just missing her new love but that she was deeply worried about him as well, no matter how hard she tried to conceal her emotions.

"Look at you two pathetic lassies." Keller addressed the ladies in his usual take-charge fashion. "The way I see it, you girls can lie around the house all day and mope, or I can drive you into the city and you can shop."

Katherine and Ashley looked at each other and smiled.

"Keller, you're the only man I know who truly really understands women. How about it, Ash? How long has it been since the O'Shea girls have invaded the designer stores of Dublin?"

Just as Ashley was about to give her approval, the door chimes rang.

"I will attend to the door; you girls get ready," ordered Keller as he shuffled his way out of the kitchen and down the corridors toward the front door.

Centuries earlier it was basically impossible for unexpected visitors to arrive to the front door of this castle or any other without an escort from the family sentries or guards, but that was not so today.

Keller had no idea what fate awaited him from behind the large wooden front door, and nothing could have prepared the family for what was about to happen next.

Keller unlatched and opened this door for the last time. Standing before him was a familiar face, a woman whom he had greeted at this same door two weeks prior, but this time she wasn't smiling. Raising her pistol, she took quick aim and dotted Keller in the forehead. He flew back and was dead before he hit the ground.

There was no wasted motion with this cold-blooded killer; once she took care of her business, she entered through the doorway, stepping over the body as if it were a discarded garment.

This tall, slender witch was not working alone, but it was quite obvious she was in charge.

Following her through door were two Middle Eastern looking thugs wielding automatic rifles. She quickly gave them hand signals, sending them running in different directions. On her headset she gave verbal commands sending two more thugs crashing through the french doors adjacent to the main kitchen, where Katherine and Ashley were still sitting.

The girls screamed with obvious terror, and the total surprise of these well-trained men left them with little time to react. Before they could run, the men were on top of them, grabbing and shoving them face down on the floor.

"Take what you want but please don't hurt us. We have little money that we keep on the premises. but I'll show you the safe," pleaded Katherine.

The request from Katherine was basically ignored by the creeps standing over them with guns. They instead continued with diligence phase two of their objective, which was binding the girls' hands and feet together with duct tape.

Now the initial shock wore off Ashley and she became filled with rage. She wasn't going to have any part of this bull crap. At least that's what she told herself. She rolled over and kicked one of the gunmen in the groin; he momentarily bent over in pain. As he was about to retaliate with the butt of his rifle to Ashley's head, a voice shouted out.

"Stop! Do not harm her, at least not yet."

The gunman immediately stood down per her orders.

Hearing a female voice, both girls looked up to see British Intelligence agent Johnson enter the room.

"You're Austin's cousin, Ivy!"

"No she's not, Mother. She is no relative of Austin. She was lying to protect her identity."

"What have you done with Keller"? Katherine cried out, sensing the worst.

"You men get them to their feet and sit them back in their chairs. Listen one time, ladies, and listen good. Nobody gets hurt if only you cooperate, and that includes talking when I'm not asking you questions. First of all, are you two the only family members here now?"

"Don't answer her, Mother."

Ivy smiled at Ashley, then walked over to her and slapped her across her face with the back of her hand, knocking her out of her chair and onto the floor.

Katherine cried out, "Please no!" as she lunged forward but was restrained by one of the men while the other put Ashley back into her chair.

Ivy tore off a piece duct tape and pasted it across Ashley's bloodied mouth.

"We are looking for Calvin McClain. If you don't want to end up like your butler, I suggest you cooperate."

Katherine shrieked and Ashley groaned after hearing this awful statement. They could only assume by Ivy's comments that their beloved Keller had been killed.

Ivy turned and walked away a few steps, touching her finger to her earpiece. Apparently she was being paged by her subordinates on her headset. She returned conversation, this time talking in Arabic, then turned to the other two gunmen in the room and barked out orders, continuing her banter in the unfamiliar tongue. The two men scrambled from the room and returned several minutes later with the other two men.

"We have completed the search, and no others are in the house."

"Did you tidy up the foyer floor?"

"Yes and disposed of the—"

"That will be all," Ivy interrupted the man before he could complete his sentence, but both girls knew exactly what they were disposing of and began sobbing uncontrollably.

"Okay then. Well let's go find Calvin."

Ivy reached behind her and pulled out a long knife from her jumpsuit, then walked over to Katherine and Ashley, now slumped over in their chairs, leaned down, and cut the heavy tape that bound their legs.

Two of the hired thugs helped the girls stand up by grabbing them under their arms and lifting them forcefully up from the floor. This did not sit well with either girl, especially, Ashley who, despite Ivy's harsh warning earlier, was ready to fight again.

This time her wiser mother held her back. Katherine immediately grabbed Ashley and held her tightly as she kicked and screamed.

Through the cruel laughter of the four hired gunmen came ice-cold orders from the evil witch commanding the raid.

"Lead them out the door. We're going to the sheep barn and if anyone, especially the younger one, tries anything, shoot her in the head. Did you understand what I said, Mother? You had better keep your daughter under control or you will lose another child."

"We will cooperate. Just don't hurt us. Please don't!"

The party was heading to the barn with the intent of a rendezvous with Calvin.

Katherine asked Ivy, "What do you want with Calvin? Please don't harm him he's just an old man. He has no money."

"Oh it's not money that we are after. It's diamonds, and your old Calvin knows just where we can find them. Now shut up and walk."

As they approached the stone barn, Ashley thought to herself, *Where is Calvin?* He had always arrived immediately in the past when she got herself in trouble, but this time she was glad he didn't arrive and was in fact hoping they wouldn't find him at all. She was not only relieved that Calvin was not up at the house but was thinking further, thank God her father and brothers were not home either, or they might have all met the same fate as Keller.

Ivy methodically spoke in Arabic when she communicated with her subordinates, as she did when they arrived at the door of the barn. Once again she barked out orders, dispersing two gunmen around the outside of the structure in different directions.

"Ladies first," directed Ivy as she pulled out her pistol and placed it in the center of Ashley's back, pushing her and Katherine through the door.

The room was as dark and quiet as it was the last time Ashley visited with Austin. This time there was a sinister feeling in the air; this feeling was in dire contrast to the spiritual aura normally experienced by the few visitors to this barn. Evil seems to seep from the pores of these greedy, murderous pigs, causing a sickly, bitter stench in the room.

Ivy motioned the men to the double door which opened into the large room filled with stalls and sheep; obviously they did not know this when they slammed through. They kicked the door open and rushed through, guns poised for the attack; however, they nearly fell over the balcony head first into the sheep. In fact, one of the men dropped his weapon into the stall below and had to have another gunman retrieve it. Ivy rushed over and evaluated the scene, conversing briefly with the other two gunmen below among the sheep before backing herself back into the room.

Embarrassed by this maneuver and the clumsiness of her troops, Ivy momentarily stepped outside of her harsh demeanor to poke fun at herself and her men.

"These Al Qaeda chaps aren't exactly British Intelligence agents, are they?"

However, the only one who found any humor in this was Ivy, and her bliss didn't last long. She took a moment to survey the room, her eyes finding the stairs then following them to the top.

"Is that Calvin's office?" Ivy asked as she nodded upward toward a lone door at the top of the stairs. Ivy didn't wait for a response. She signaled her henchmen to start climbing but then stopped them.

Ivy stood there for a moment, staring intensely at the door as if she was studying her next move, then turned to the girls.

"Ashley, call for him. Tell him you are here with visitors."

"Oh trust me; he already knows you are here."

Katherine's matter-of-fact comment sent a chill through Ivy even though she didn't outwardly show it. Ivy accepted

Katherine's commentary as fact and went back to plan A, allowing her men to storm up the steps.

In single file the men went up the steps with the two O'Shea women, with Ivy bringing up the rear. When they reached the top, Ivy stuck her gun directly behind Ashley's ear, then nodded for the men to open the door. This time the door wasn't locked and the door effortlessly swung open, readying the room to receive its new callers.

Calvin was not there. The room was empty of any apparent human form but not empty of life. Virtually at the same time as they entered the room, so did the rays of sunlight shining through the stained-glass window, illuminating the entire room. This was the same occurrence previously experienced by Ashley and Austin on their visit.

One of the men, named Amid, approached the table in the center of the room and was about to wipe out the communion set centered in the middle with his arm when Ivy screamed at him.

"Stop, you are not to touch anything unless I command!"

She repeated this order in Arabic, this time slower and with less zeal.

Bang! The door behind them slammed shut and they could hear the lock engage.

The door slamming and locking for no explainable reason got everyone in the room's attention. Fueling the chaos was the sunlight through the stained window, which now seamed to intensify, creating a virtual kaleidoscope, sending the two men into a mild panic. They rushed over to the door to find it locked, confirming what they had just witnessed. Shouting in Arabic, the men poised their rifles, ready to shoot their way through the door, when all of a sudden the door unlocked itself and opened about six inches.

Ivy sensed she needed to immediately regain control of the situation or she would lose two of her four men. As they were about to go running out the door, she fired her gun in the ceiling, immediately stopping them in their tracks.

"All right, Calvin, we have had enough of your little tricks. If you don't show yourself immediately, I'm going to blow a hole in the back of dear Katherine's head. If you wish to play games like a child, I will oblige you. If you're not standing before me by the time I count to ten, then you lose and so does Katherine.

"One, two, three…"

Things became more tense as she announced "six." Ivy grabbed Katherine by the nape of her neck and held the gun up to her head. Ashley darted toward Katherine but was immediately intercepted by one of the thugs.

"I'm not kidding, Calvin. Seven, eight…"

Ivy positioned herself behind Katherine, grabbed her hair, and pushed her head forward, pulling the hammer back on the gun as she pressed it harder against the back of Katherine's head.

"Nine!"

A mournful but commanding voice filled the room like the melancholy melody of a pipe organ inside a cathedral.

"Release Mrs. O'Shea and put away the gun now! There's no need for more violence, missy. Your British brutality sickens me to no end."

Everyone was so focused on Ivy's next horrific move and looking toward the door, expecting Calvin to enter, that no one noticed him sitting with his dog in the corner of the room behind them. Seemingly out of thin air, Calvin had appeared. The gunmen and Ivy were dumbfounded, so much so that it was several seconds before Ivy could grasp the situation and respond.

"Are ya all right, ma'am? I'm sorry I couldn't have stopped this violence, but don't worry about Keller. Heaven has welcomed him in with open arms. He's very happy he's now joined his family, who were anxiously waiting his arrival."

"Enough of this heartwarming crap. My patience is at its limit. My men have searched all over this damn country, and even I, with the unsuspecting help of a bungling CIA agent, have turned over every blarney stone looking for this needle in a haystack, but no more. Calvin, I was hoping I wouldn't have to resort to violence as you said, but I couldn't wait for that naval special forces chap to find those diamonds. After listening to conversations from Austin's bugged phone, I found out a pleasant surprise. We don't need to do anymore hunting. You, Calvin, know where the diamonds are. You see, I don't intend on waiting for Austin to eventually figure out the diamonds' hiding spot. There is no reason to wait any longer. I just need to persuade Calvin here to tell me or show me where the tears of

Mary are right now, and then my men and I will be gone and no one else will get hurt."

Ivy looked around the room and spotted the steamer trunk in the corner. She motioned for one of her men to open it, but when he approached the trunk Calvin's dog began to snarl.

"What do you have in the trunk, Calvin? Your dog seems very protective of it. I don't suppose it's the diamonds, is it?"

"Dog biscuits." Calvin's quick wit drew a smile from Ivy even though it wasn't intended for its levity.

"Well what are you waiting for; drag it out and open it up," Ivy ordered her subordinate, who hesitated when the dog started growling.

Turning away from the dog and refocusing on the trunk, the man bent over and grabbed the handles on the side and the dog went ballistic. It broke free from Calvin's grip and darted across the room toward the now terrified Islamic fanatic.

Tat, tat, tat! the sound rang out from the automatic rifle, followed by the sickening dull thud of the lifeless animal as it hit the floor.

There was a moment of eerie silence. The girls were in shock over what had just happened. The fanatical gunman was completely without remorse—almost smug about what he had just done.

"You bastard," cried Ashley.

Calvin stood up and walked over to the stained-glass window. Reaching up, he picked out a key, cleverly camouflaged by the mosaic stained pane. Gathering himself, he then turned and walked over to the trunk, leaned over, and with all eyes and guns in the room tracing his every move, he unlocked the chest. Calvin gently raised the lid and rested it against the wall. Reaching inside, he pulled out a beautiful handmade quilt and unfolded it as he walked over to the remains of his former lifelong companion, who lay lifeless on the floor. With a loving motion, Calvin kneeled down and covered his friend, then mumbled a prayer and made a sign of the cross and stood up.

"Please, no more violence. If your evil desire is to know where the diamonds are, then I shall tell you, but be warned your foolish greed will be the sword by which you will die."

"Evil desires maybe, but greed, never. Greed is a weakness of fools and you will find, Calvin, I'm neither weak nor a fool. Yes, many people, including those at the top of British Intelligence, will find out this soon as well. They made a big mistake with me by not respecting my talents. Oh yes, a big mistake. Fortunately there are those out there who do respect me and recognize my talents, and are willing to pay a premium to have me on their side.

"You all have no idea. The diamonds mean nothing to me, but snatching them away right under the nose of British and U.S. Intelligence, then trading them for plutonium, well now that, Calvin, Katherine, and Ashley…that means sweet revenge."

Ashley shook her head.

"Well I seem to have gotten carried away. Calvin, you say you have something to tell me?"

Calvin reached down in the chest under more quilts and pulled out a very old piece of parchment in the shape of a shamrock, and he began to read the inscription.

"The father, the son, and the Holy Ghost. My Saint Patrick had very little possessions throughout his life and this is one of the very few, and the only one that wasn't buried with his remains. What you seek, however, is the gift which belonged to Mary Magdalene. It now lies beside Patrick beneath the granite rock marking his grave.

"I had a feeling it was entombed somewhere, but I couldn't go digging up every saint's grave we would come upon. We were making the papers enough with our activities of searching the churches, and of course there was the untidy elimination of those two Asians that caused quite the stir. Saint Patrick's grave, you say. Damn, I was just there."

Ivy took a moment to reflect.

"That is one hell of a rock. We need to move to get to the sarcophagus.

"Amid, you will go to Downpatrick and obtain a mobile crane or some piece of heavy equipment, chains, and shovels, whatever. We are running out of time. I don't care how you get what we need. Steal it if must, but have it there tomorrow night.

"We don't have the luxury of totally casing the place before we hit; however, I know all the tourists will be gone after ten p.m., so we will make our move after midnight.

"The rest of you, listen up. I don't like this, but we are going to remain here over night. You had better hope that the rest of your family doesn't decide to come home tonight."

"You had better hope that Austin doesn't come here and find you, Ms. Johnson," snapped Ashley.

"Oh yes, your Navy Seal boyfriend. Aren't you cute. I should have never missed when I shot at him in that damn bell tower. Oh don't worry, missy. I won't miss him again, and if you don't shut that big mouth of yours you will be waiting for him when he arrives in heaven."

Amid, apparently the only thug who spoke English, was second in command of Ivy's gang; he immediately took off after receiving his orders. The other three received their instructions in Arabic. Then two of them left the room, not to be seen again until the morning.

Ivy paced the floor all night with a guard at the door while Katherine and Ashley slept as best they could with their heads on the table. Calvin, however, sat and rocked in his chair, stopping occasionally to ask Ivy questions. She, for the most part, was ignoring him, but his persistence was wearing on her nerves. Ivy had warned Calvin not to pull any funny business or she would shoot the women. She probably would have shot Calvin just for being a nuisance, but she wasn't sure he was telling her the truth about the diamonds' location and she might need him again, so she endured his obnoxious interruptions.

The morning finally came after what seemed an eternity to Ashley and Katherine. The shock and horror of yesterday was like a bad dream. Upon their awakening, reality was quickly realized when Ivy demanded their attention.

Ivy addressed her men first before turning to her hostages.

"Listen up. This is what's going to happen. Ashley and I are going to Saul. Katherine and Calvin are staying here for insurance. Calvin, if anything that you have told me turns out to be false, I won't take any mercy on this girl. Is this perfectly clear?"

"Quite clear," muttered Calvin.

"When we get the diamonds, and only when we get the diamonds, I will phone my man here and he will leave you and I will turn Ashley loose. Oh and as far as funny business goes here, you have already witnessed Omar's quick gun work on that mutt lying on the floor. He's just waiting to have the opportunity to kill something else, so if I were you I would be very careful."

CHAPTER 33:

Bryan turned out to be a big help. He actually was quite knowledgeable about Saint Patrick and would drive me up and down the coastline, showing me churches and monasteries believed to be started by Patrick or one of his close followers. Bryan was very enthusiastic about helping me and never questioned my interest in Saint Patrick. He actually was a bigger help than his cousin, just not as pretty, and believe it or not, we were beginning to communicate with each other very well.

I even asked him if he had ever heard of the the tears of Mary but he had not. I think he thought I was talking about a novel, because later that day he drove me to a used book store.

My several logged hours of surveillance of Slane Hill was basically over. Nothing out of the ordinary had happened since my attack. This whole adventure was beginning to bore me and I know the boys out on the water had to be going insane. *I feel that I should be doing more than I have been but I'm not sure what. This whole thing seems crazy even Kenny and the CIA have no clue as what to do or where to look. Hell, they don't even know if the diamonds are even still in Ireland.*

Today Bryan and I were driving back from one of our little trips up the coast. Bryan has a surprisingly beautiful voice. He was singing an old Irish hymn that he told me he had learned as a child. While Bryan serenaded and drove, I stared out the window, daydreaming about Ashley, wishing she was still here with me.

Ring! Ring!

My satellite phone had been ringing with more regularity lately. This time it was Boomer calling just to chat.

"Been shot at today, Father Brock?"

"Well if it isn't my oversized seafaring friend. How's the fishing?"

"Fishing sucks and so does the boredom of waiting for you to find those damn bad guys. Hey, by the way, I thought you Seal guys were tough. How did you let that shooter get away?"

"I don't know, man. Whoever squeezed off those rounds at me was flat-out fast. I mean, it was like they just flew. I ran track in school and I was the fastest bud in Seal boot camp, so I'm no turtle, and I couldn't even get close enough to get a shot off."

"Runners. Does everyone in the world today run but me? Hell even that damn limey British Intelligence chick ran every day. Kenny said she was some Olympic track star or something. What a bitch she was."

"What did you say, Boomer?"

"I said she was a bitch!"

"No, before that. Did you say she Agent Johnson was an Olympic sprinter?"

"World class. My football career might have been extended a few more years only if I could have had some of her speed."

"Yeah, whatever. Where is Johnson?"

"Haven't seen her since I got thrown in the Irish pokey. I guess she is off the case. Why? Hey. what are you thinking?"

"I don't know. Is Kenny there? Let me speak to him."

"He's not here; the dog went to shore. English-side CIA business or something."

"You think she's your shooter, don't you?"

"Kenny will be back tomorrow. I will fill him in on our conversation, we will check her out. There was something about her that bothered me all along, interesting enough."

Before Boomer hung up, he suggested I go back to the tower and extract one of the bullets lodged in the woodwork. They would make arrangements to get the bullet picked up and would do a lab test to determine what kind of gun was used. British agents only use certain issued automatic weapons. It was a long shot, but hell, everything we were doing had been a long shot.

Obviously Bryan heard every word between Boomer and I and he understood well enough to know we were talking about a female who ran.

Bryan told me—well, as best I could interpret his thick brogue, that is—that right after Ashley and I arrived at his house, an English woman checked in alone. She was apparently very rude and sarcastic. She even told him not to stand so close to her until he bathed.

"You don't think I smell, do you Austin?"

"Uh, well you know how some women are. Don't you, Bryan?"

"Oh fiddlesticks." He sighed momentarily before continuing to tell me she, like his cousin, was a runner. In fact, she left to run early in the morning, right after Ashley. He found it amusing they were dressed almost identically. He was going to introduce them but she checked out almost immediately after she returned from her run.

Bryan was trying to remember her name.

"I think it was Myra or something. I can check my log when we get back. No, I remember. It was Myrna Wilson."

So after we returned home I ran up the hill one more time and was able to find and dig out with my knife one of the rounds lodged in the doorframe.

While walking back down the mountain, carrying the bullet that almost took my life, I called Boomer on the two-way satellite phone to tell him that I was successful in finding a bullet to check, and also I needed them to check out the name Myrna Wilson.

Boomer said that after we had talked earlier he immediately got in touch with Kenny, and he told me to be alert to his arrival tomorrow morning.

"Austin, the more I thought about the possibility of Agent Johnson being dirty, the more it got me thinking. I was beginning to wonder if she had set up that little police raid in Dublin that conveniently blew my cover and got me deported. Come to think of it, she did a lot of listening to your bugged phone. I told her we weren't there to spy on you, just watch your back. Her response was for me basically to kiss off."

"Well, let's not condemn Agent Johnson just yet before we have any hard evidence. I'll talk to you later, Boomer. My phone is going dead."

When I got back to the house, Bryan had a big plate of Irish stew waiting on me. Singing wasn't his only talent. That was the best stew I think I've ever eaten. I thought to myself, *Bryan would make some woman a good husband.* He just needed a little help with his appearance. *Oh well, who am I kidding. He needs a lot of help with his appearance, but he has a heart of gold and that's what's most important.*

After I finished eating, I asked Bryan if I could use his phone to call Ashley.

"No answer, not even Keller," I said out loud as so Bryan could hear.

"Maybe they all went for a drive or something. If you don't mind, Bryan. I would like to try again later. Perhaps I'll wait until the morning. I think I might turn in for this evening. Good night."

"Sleep well, my American friend."

CHAPTER 34:

I retired to my room. By the way, it was not the same room I'd had prior my visit from the intruder. I took another room mainly for the precautionary reason of enforcing the illusion that I had checked out and left town and the fact that my new room had a much more comfortable bed.

When my head hit the pillow I was out for the night, well almost.

Just before sunrise I got a visit from my old friend from above, Abraham.

I was sound asleep, which is rare for me. Since becoming a Seal, I have adapted myself to sleeping light. Nevertheless, I arose from my bed thinking we were having an earthquake and found myself immersed in white light. It was the same extreme brilliance as I experienced the on the other occasions, but this time Abraham was shaking the end of my bed, trying to awaken me; thus the earthquake.

"Wake up, my son. You have much to do. Evil has come to take the gift, the tears of Mary, and more innocents will die, including the one you love, unless you act quick. The gift will always be safe, but those who stand between evil and the gift will perish at the hands of this evil."

"Is Ashley in trouble? I need to go to her now!"

"No, my son, she will come to you, escorted by this evil."

"Go to a place they call Saul, to the grave of Patrick, and wait. I cannot help you any further, but rely on my friend, the keeper of the sheep. Calvin has special abilities given to him from heaven, abilities given to only a chosen few. God will be with you."

With those departing words, my body went numb and I fell back into bed. The bright light left and so did Abraham. It seemed as if I was in some sort of a mild coma until the morning sunlight broke through the thin cotton curtains hanging from the window.

I jumped from my bed, hopping on one leg as I pulled on my pants. By the time I arrived at the stairs at the end of the hall, I had accelerated to a full sprint. My feet barely touched the steps as I descended the staircase. Bryan thought the house was on fire when he saw me heading for the pantry, donning only my pants and running at full speed.

"What's wrong, Austin?"

I grabbed the phone that sat on the corner coffee table and began pounding out Ashley and Katherine's number. I listened as it rang and rang.

"Bryan, can you get me to Saint Patrick's tomb in Saul, Downpatrick? Katherine and Ashley are in big trouble."

Bryan, not saying another word, left the room while I redialed the O'Sheas. He returned momentarily, holding a shotgun in one hand and a backpack in the other. He lifted the backpack, looked at me, and said; "left over IRA."

While Bryan got the car ready I ran back upstairs and finished dressing, packed my bag, and loaded my gun. As we drove off I called on my sat phone. This time Kenny answered.

"Kenny, I think something's going down. I can't explain why but I'm heading for Saul and I need someone to go to the O'Shea castle right away. I've got a bad feeling. I left a bullet for you of the shooter in an envelope by the phone downstairs where I'm staying."

"I don't think we need it. I talked to Chief Inspector Smyth. Myrna Wilson and Ivy Johnson are the same person and she is supposed to be on holiday in Greece."

"Listen, Austin, we both don't want to jump to conclusions yet. Right now Ivy Johnson's only a person of interest. Her being still in Ireland and not in Greece doesn't make her the shooter; nor does it mean she's after the diamonds. Okay, now that I said that, it doesn't look good for her.

"Here's the quick down-and-dirty. Right after Boomer got a hold of me, I called Smyth, who really was reluctant to discuss his agent with me until I mentioned the name Myrna Wilson. I knew I got his attention. There was a long pause before Smyth told me he had to call me back. Thirty minutes later he did, and here is what he said.

"Ivy Johnson was due back from her supposed little vacation three days ago to report for a new assignment. Instead a letter showed up to her immediate superior explaining she had a death in her family and she needed additional time off. They tried to get in touch with her but were unable, and now as of last night they are physically trying to track her down.

"Ms. Johnson was selected by the British secret service at a time when their popular belief was to recruit intelligent athletes, and she was exactly that. Johnson was an Olympian sprinter at Oxford. The knock on her was she had a horrible temper and a contemptuous sadistic nature; the other athletes hated her immensely. The agency knew they had their hands full but felt they could harness her nasty traits and turn her into the perfect agent.

"Johnson in fact did become the perfect agent; she was slated to receive a substantial promotion which would have almost doubled her salary. However, because of—let's just say— chauvinistic politics, she was overlooked. The timeline was about fourteen months ago. She was posing undercover as a European arms dealer, her alias Myrna Wilson. Wilson (or Johnson) had just purchased handheld surface-to-air missiles from an arms dealer in Yemen with the hope of building their trust to go for the bigger prize.

"According to Smyth's intelligence, this Yemen group had a small cache of plutonium that they apparently smuggled out of the former USSR and were now cautiously trying to move on the black market.

"Apparently they were so close to nailing this group, but something spooked the Yemen group and they went back into their hole.

"This happened shortly after Smyth called to give her the bad news.

"Smyth was concerned over how Johnson would take the news, but he thought she handled it well, considering.

"Austin, two days ago a suspicious super yacht with accompanying jet helicopter joined us out here. They are anchored about two miles from our position. Coincidently this particular yacht is registered to a group of Yemen businessmen. And I'm guessing I know what business they are in.

"Austin, before your phone goes dead, I thought I would let you know I called Admiral Higgins before calling you. This thing is getting big enough to require a little heavier backup.

"Austin, if you think Johnson is at the O'Shea castle, why are you going to Saul?"

"Let's just say I have my own intelligence. You will just have to trust me on this. I think Johnson has Ashley and he is taking her to Saul; Saint Patrick's tomb of all places. I need someone to go to the castle just to be sure. I can't be in both places at once."

"Austin, I'm waiting to be briefed on more intelligence regarding this plutonium. I am told it may be conflicting to what the Brits have told us. I will call you back soon."

We pulled around a large pay- loader sitting parallel the curb of the street, then into the parking lot of the cathedral. After finding a parking spot, we got out. I looked at Bryan and he looked at me. Now what? There was a tremendous crowd of vacationing pilgrims filing in line to see the large granite gravestone directly over the famous saint's remains.

We fell in line with the rest of the people, both of us scanning the crowd. There was no sign of Ashley and no one was acting suspicious. After about fifteen minutes in line, we finally reached the rock. I have to admit there was a humbling, almost reverent feeling when we got next to the stone. We circled the rock once, admiring the flowers and personal notes deposited there by pilgrims. Bryan kissed the rock and crossed his heart before we exited the scene and entered the museum. Obviously the last thing on my mind was meandering through a museum looking at artifacts, but that's where the flow of the crowd took me, so I went. Tourists. I was in the middle of a sea of humanity. If Ashley was here it would be hard to believe she would be in any trouble, unless she was being trampled. However, this was where Abraham instructed me to go and he was quite clear about it. He told me to go to the grave and wait, so that's what we will do.

Bryan insisted on staying, even though I told him he didn't need to. In a scolding voice he reminded me that Ashley was his cousin and that a man of any worth would always be there for a family member in trouble. Well, at least that's what I interpreted him to say.

We parked ourselves underneath a tree several feet away from the grave but with a good vantage point of all who walked by it. The hours clicked by and the crowd slowly began diminishing. I interrupted Bryan's humming to ask him a question.

"So, Bryan, if you were Saint Patrick and you had something very dear and valuable to you and you wished to hide this very dear and valuable something possibly for eternity or at least the eternity here on Earth, where would you hide this something?"

I was totally expecting Bryan to give me one of those "what the heck are you trying to say to me" looks, but instead, without hesitation, he fired back, "I would take it with me to my grave, laddy!"

"Precisely what I was thinking, Mary Magdalene took them to her grave and so did Patrick."

"Took what. Austin?"

"It's a long story, but I have a feeling you might find out what 'what' is later."

The sun was setting in the west, and caretakers had started policing the grounds, picking up debris. Bryan and I sitting off by ourselves began to stick out. Being a good special forces operative especially on reconnaissance (and basically that's what we were doing) meant adapting and blending in to our surroundings—being stealthy. Our background or surroundings changed from what they were earlier. We were now not able to blend in, so to speak. I told Bryan we needed to leave along with the rest of the people or at least make the appearance we were leaving and come back once the last employee had left.

We drove out of the parking lot, heading down the road about a kilometer or so, then doubled back, parking about a block or so away from the entrance, still close enough that we could see at least the parking area and parts of the grounds with field glasses.

I grabbed my duffel bag from behind the seat. Reaching inside, I pulled out my camo face paint and my black shirt and camouflaged paints. I set my nine millimeter on the dash of the car and began to change. Without hesitance, Bryan took the paint and began applying it to his face, then looked at me and stated boldly and emphatically, "Semper fi!"

"Well, not exactly my branch of the United States armed service, but I think I understand your enthusiasm. The first thing you need to do is lose that white T-shirt. Dingy as it is, it will still look like a billboard if you wear it out there at night. I really need you to stay put here in the car and watch my back. You can signal me if someone enters by the street. I will position myself in a place where I can see both the granite rock and your car. Just flash your lights to alert me the minute you see someone or something."

Bryan nodded his head, acknowledging my instructions and got out of the car, the same time as me. He took off his shirt and threw it in the trunk, then retrieved his shotgun and bag of goodies, and returned to his post behind the wheel. Before I disappeared in the background, I looked back to see Bryan applying camo paint to his lily-white chest and belly. I laughed, thinking to myself he was less conspicuous and better off wearing his dirty T-shirt

CHAPTER 35:

The museum was well-illuminated by the night security lights, which also cast a halo out over the nearby granite tomb. Because of the well-lit area and the three-quarter moon, I didn't need my night vision goggles, but the trick was not for me to easily see others; it was for others not to easily see me.

I did find myself an advantage, so to speak, in the shadows, high enough in elevation that I could just make out Bryan's car and also well within range to take out someone standing at the rock with my gun if I needed to.

For more than an hour or so I focused back and forth between the rock and the car. Suddenly a shadow appeared hunched over, running between trees, carrying a rifle. The silhouette was of a large male; his clumsy jerky movements made him an easy target to spot. I trained my pistol and moved slowly toward his direction. As I got closer, I noticed the familiar black-and-white markings of one fat Irishman running with a shotgun in his hand. I was boiling mad. Bryan was on the verge of blowing my cover. Why didn't he stay put like I ordered? I was working my way toward him as fast as I could, weaving in and out through the shadows, hoping like hell I could get to him first, before he was spotted. About fifty meters away from me, ringing his neck, I heard Bryan yell "freeze." There in the dimly lit archway to the museum Bryan had the drop on a man in a black leather coat and wool cap. Bryan's advantage quickly changed. The man spun around, grabbing the barrel of the shotgun, and delivered a blow simultaneously to Bryan's abdomen with his knee. In the blink of the eye the tables had turned. Bryan was now on the ground, staring up the barrel of his own gun, which was now held contentiously by the stranger. The few seconds while this scuffle was taking place allowed me to cover the fifty meters undetected, and now it was my turn to take the upper hand.

"Drop the shotgun!"

I firmly pressed the barrel of my gun against the back of the stranger's head, just beside his ear, and braced my legs, anticipating a possible countermove. In the background I heard Bryan saying over and over, "Sorry. I'm sorry. I should have flashed the lights."

The man flinched initially when the cold steel met his scull, but he now stood perfectly still, so I figured he was sizing up his next move.

I was one second away from dropping him after he ignored my second request to drop the gun. Then I heard a familiar voice.

"Stand down, sailor!"

Hiding in the shadows, eclipsed from my view until exposing himself by moving up to meet my peripheral vision, was agent Kenny.

I momentarily took my eye off my target for a quick glance over my shoulder to confirm it was indeed who I thought it was, but I was not quite ready to relinquish my position.

"Kenny, this man standing in front of me in a most precarious position wouldn't happen to be British agent Smyth."

"You wouldn't shoot an ally, now would you, Austin?"

"You mean an unannounced ally like you. Aren't you Brits familiar with the term *friendly fire?*"

"Point taken! So does this apologetic chap on the ground belong to you, Austin?"

"Yes, I suppose. Up until now he's been a big help."

I stood down and relaxed my weapon, as did Agent Smyth. Smyth extended his hand and helped Bryan to his feet, then gave him back his shotgun.

Smyth couldn't resist getting in one more jab at Bryan and me by asking if I taught Bryan the intricacies of applying camouflage paint American-style. Kenny and Smyth were the only one's finding that amusing.

"What are you guys doing here? You laugh at Bryan, but you are the numbskulls who waltz right in the middle of my stakeout. You could have blown my cover, and still could by standing here. Kenny, did you send someone to the O'Shea castle?"

"Don't worry, son. Agent Gibson and his men along with Boomer have secured the castle. I will fill you in inside."

"Did you say Boomer!"

"In light of the new information that has surfaced, Smyth has the full cooperation of the Irish, which also includes, among other things, allowing Boomer King back in the country."

"What new information?"

Smyth dipped into his pocket and pulled out a key, then preceded to unlock the door to the museum. Kenny followed him through the door, then Bryan and finally me.

My question wasn't immediately answered; however, I felt that I was about to get a full briefing. After disengaging the alarm control panel, Smyth led us by flashlight up the stairs; no lights were turned on for obvious reasons. On the second level was a conference room with windows overlooking the grounds. It was a perfect place to observe but a tough place in which to react quickly.

Kenny and I started closing blinds as the other two pulled up some chairs.

"First off, Austin, I don't know who your shotgun-toting partner is, but I know he isn't ready to hear classified information. So unless you want us to shoot him when we are finished, you better have him stand out in the hall."

"Well a few minutes ago I would have had you shoot him, but...Bryan, do you mind?"

"Yes, sir. I have learned my lesson. No more disobedience from me," sputtered Bryan.

"And close the door behind you," added Kenny.

I pulled out my flashlight from my back pocket and handed it to Bryan to light his path across the room and through the door.

As soon as Bryan closed the door, Kenny began talking, with the three of us sitting in the dark and peering out the window through the slits in the blinds.

"Seaman Brock, if we had more time I would remove you from this case, but we don't. Admiral Higgins is furious over how we the CIA have been handling this mission, and I can't blame him. Our intelligence is lousy. Even verifying the intelligence of the English is slow and archaic, as you will find out in a minute.

"You have basically achieved your mission. Correct me if I'm wrong, but we are probably staring down at the resting place of the tears of Mary and the bad guys are close behind.

"Normally at this time you would be free to return to your naval unit; however, our main objective has just gotten a little more complex according to British commander Smyth. After our conversation this morning, Austin, I got a visit from the man to your right. He informs me that early British Intelligence was wrong. Now he is ready to share with us all the English know and all they now speculate, so, Smyth, you better talk fast before Johnson and the others show up.

"The reports that plutonium was smuggled out of the former USSR," Kenny continued, "and purchased by a Saudi oil baron to be used for negotiation for the tears of Mary, if found, turned out to be false. There are lots of cases or speculations of unaccountable plutonium from the former country. There is this Saudi that has been very vocal about his aspirations of acquiring the diamonds, but we now strongly believe he has no plutonium.

"So this leads me to tell you about our embarrassment—our dirty little secret, if I must. We British, like you Americans, prefer to handle our problems internally without asking for help, but this time our problem was exposed. Our rogue agent, Ms. Ivy Johnson, alias Myrna Wilson, is turning out to have been totally underestimated as well as being undiscovered by our internal investigation people.

"Quickly let me start from the beginning with a brief history as it relates to our situation.

"Sellafield, perhaps you are familiar with it. Sellafield is one of England's largest nuclear sites located on the coast of the Irish Sea in Cambria. The Sellafield site was built on the former nuclear site named after the nearby village Windscale. Windscale developed the first British weapon-grade plutonium production facility in the late 1940s. Efforts were in full force through the '50s and '60s to build England's 'big bomb.' The site has been much maligned with controversy over the years, mostly because of discharges of radioactive material into the Irish Sea. After the cold war, efforts were made to try to change the image of the now renamed Sellafield site, focusing mainly on energy—nuclear power.

"Now this is where I begin to explain to you the relevancy of all this. About ten years ago the plant confidentially reported to us of their internal discovery of approximately thirty kilograms—

184

that's about sixty-five pounds—of unaccounted-for plutonium. That's enough plutonium to make seven nuclear bombs. This little incident remains top secret even today.

"We interrogated and investigated the employees for months, with most of our efforts concentrated on the head scientist in charge of that particular area. He had always insisted that the missing plutonium was only missing on paper, that it was nothing more than a clerical mistake. The plutonium never surfaced; nor did any evidence of wrongdoing. Finally about three years ago the head scientist in charge passed away.

"After his death we basically shelved this investigation, never connecting the dots until now.

"Gentlemen, the name of the head scientist was Wilson, Dr. Eugene Wilson. The thing we missed about Agent Johnson, which causes us the most embarrassment, was that her mother's maiden name was Wilson; in fact, I now recall her telling me that she selected her alias after her grandmother, Myrna Wilson. It was just recently confirmed to me that the much maligned Dr. Wilson was the grandfather of one Ivy Johnson.

"Remember I said it was just confirmed to me. Apparently my superiors chose not to bore me with this little detail. Consequently this was the real reason why Johnson was denied her promotion, even though their reason for denial was never revealed to her.

"Gentlemen, it gets better. Dr. Wilson was an avid sailor and was known for spending his off days on his small ketch sailing the coast. His coworkers noted in their reports to the investigation panel that they noticed he abruptly stopped sailing. Wilson's reply to the board when asked indicated that his yacht sank in an unpredicted storm, but it goes on to state that he produced no evidence to support his claim. The investigators for whatever reason did not pursue this.

"Ivy's parents died in an automobile accident when she was very young. Being an only child, she was raised by her grandparents, Eugene and Myrna. She excelled at sports, especially track and field. Even when competing against men she was quite superior. She caught the eyes of many universities, including Oxford, where she accepted an athletic scholarship. As an Olympian she turned out to be one of the college's favored daughters, but with her awful temper she quickly fell from their graces.

"Well, you now have a little history and background of Ms. Johnson and her grandfather. I will tell you what I believe to be my synopsis of this whole mater. Mind you, it's merely based upon circumstantial as well as unsubstantiated conclusions, but I am afraid that's all we have at this moment.

"I believe that Dr. Wilson took the plutonium from Windscale, packed it securely in air-tight containers, stole it away on his yacht, sailed to a predetermined location, then sank his boat, later to be raised by a diver, then sold on the black market. Dr. Wilson's 'later' never came. He succumbed to cancer before he could complete phase two of his plan. I also believe that he told Ivy the coordinates of this sunken treasure, perhaps on his death bed.

"Agent Ivy Johnson holds all the aces; she has masterfully put together a most intriguing plan. So a review of the players involved in her little charade is as follows: a wealthy Saudi who wants desperately to possess the tears of Mary diamonds (and my guess is he's funding her totally), a super yacht filled with Islamic fundamentalists from Yemen sympathetic to any terror group willing to pay the maximum price for plutonium, plutonium that they still seek to obtain from Johnson, and of course there is us, the two most revered intelligence organizations in the world. What anger this girl must have inside her and what a waste of talent.

"Well, gentlemen, the British Navy is in position to take out the Yemen yacht if necessary. However there is not anything we can do until they break some law.

"Obviously the recovery of the plutonium is our first priority, over anything else. If we can keep the diamonds buried, then that would be a bonus."

Well I didn't give a damn how angry that girl was inside; this U.S. Navy Seal was getting really pissed, and my priority was the recovery of the innocent she held hostage.

CHAPTER 36:

The atmosphere in the barn at O'Shea Castle earlier that same morning was surreal—that is until the familiar buzz of a helicopter caught the attention of Ivy as she finished doling out her orders to her men.

"Oh yes. By that sound I believe that our ride is here. Get up, Ashley, it's time for us to go dig up some diamonds."

Both Ashley and Katherine rose to their feet. Katherine's eyes filled with tears as she gave her daughter a long, concerned hug.

"Don't worry, Mother. I will be back before Calvin can finish one of his stories."

"I don't know about that, missy. Ya know my stories can be quite long sometimes."

Calvin stood up after his reply, then winked at Ashley, walked over, and put his arm around Katherine to comfort her.

"Please don't fret, Mrs. O'Shea. These evil people will find what they are looking for, then Ms Ashley will return and this nightmare will be over."

Ivy grabbed Ashley by the arm and escorted her out of the room, leaving a machine-gun-toting thug behind to watch the two other hostages. Down the steps and through the door of the barn to an awaiting helicopter, Ivy pulled Ashley.

From upstairs inside Calvin's room they listened as the dull thumping of the blades of the helicopter, which increased to a loud buzz. Then the buzz seemed to climb up the wall and over the roof. The buzz faded to a hum that finally muted to silence.

The jet-powered gunship flew over the rocky hillside and treetops like a cruise missle.

"So what's your hurry to get to Saul," shouted Ashley over the noise of the chopper. :You said we weren't to be at the grave till midnight."

Ivy hesitated momentarily before answering.

"My dear, you are on a need-to-know basis. Oh what the hell. I suppose it doesn't mater. If you must know, we need to make a stop first to pick up a couple of packages. Have you ever done any island hopping? I need to pick up some sunken treasure. Not to worry. I have already hired a couple of saps to do my diving for me. We just need to recover it. Now shut up and be a good little girl and enjoy the ride."

Ashley wasn't accustomed to being bullied or patronized like she had been for the last twenty-four hours by this English witch. Growing up with older brothers, she learned at an early age not to put with any bullcrap or she would continue to receive it. This time was different. Her brothers weren't cold-blooded killers; nevertheless Ashley was convinced she would find the opportunity to get her revenge.

For the remainder of the trip Ashley stared out the window and thought about Austin, hoping and praying he would somehow find her in Saul.

"Calvin, for years I've listened to the men tell stories at the breakfast table or in front of the fireplace. The tears of Mary indeed, nothing more than Irish Catholic folklore, at least that's what I told myself and my children," Katherine said.

"Calvin, do the tears of Mary really exist?"

"Yes, Katherine. They are as real as your blue eyes."

"And you have you seen them?"

"Oh no, my lady; I'm not worthy, but someday if my lord allows…. You see, it's not the diamonds that radiate beauty; it's what the diamonds represent."

The banter back and forth between Katherine and Calvin irritated their captor; he slammed the butt of his riffle on the table, then shook his head and wagged his finger to indicate his displeasure at their conversation. This evil soldier could not speak a word of English, so he quickly ended any conversation that he couldn't understand.

About every hour the guards would rotate. The outside guard would relieve the inside one and so forth. This went on throughout the morning. Around noon the relief guard brought some food, which he had raided from the house's main kitchen. There was not much dialogue between the two men. They were clearly not friends; they were just performing a mission and nothing more.

Nearly two hours went by and there was no switch. The guard that was in the room was pacing the floor and repeatedly looking at his watch. Finally he pulled out his handheld two-way radio, keyed it, and sent out a vernacular spray of Arabic, basically saying "Where the hell are you?!" There was no reply from his comrade, so he keyed the mike and repeated, this time with more anger in his voice.

Calvin and Katherine at this point were very cognizant of their frustrated captor. Calvin turned and winked at Katherine as if to indicate to her that perhaps this was the beginning of a meltdown.

Suddenly there was a light tapping on the door. *Tap, tap, tap.* Immediately the angered gunman darted to the door, preparing to chew out his insubordinate counterpart. He grabbed the latch and with one swift movement pulled the door open. What a surprise it was for that Islamic creep to introduce his face to a jumbo-sized ex-NFL lineman's fist. He went flying across the room like a turd being shot out of cannon. The crumpled gunman quickly recovered and grabbed his riffle, but as he straightened to fire he let out a bloodcurdling scream and dropped his weapon. His hands were burnt severely by the stock of his gun. Now totally bewildered, he looked up and was greeted once more—this time by the butt of an M-16. This final blow delivered to the gunman rendered him down for the count, and out cold.

"My name is Jim King. You can call me Boomer. I'm with U.S. Central Intelligence Agency."

Boomer looked over at the two excited bystanders and then reached down to handcuff the gunman. Before slapping on the cuffs, Boomer examined the blisters on the man's palms.

"What did you guys do to his gun? Whatever it was it burnt the hell out of his hands and may have saved my life."

During this episode, which lasted a mere few seconds, Katherine and Calvin scurried to the corner of the room, where they were still huddled.

"Well, I'm all done here. Hey, there are a four excited O'Shea men waiting patiently outside ready to see you two. So what the heck are you waiting on?"

"What about Ashley, my daughter. Is she downstairs with my husband?"

"No, ma'am, after we secured the area and took out our initial threat, we searched the house with your husband and brothers before coming down here. We assumed Ashley might be with you."

"I believe young Miss Ashley left with others in a helicopter about seven hours ago; we were not expecting her to be in the house. Mrs. O'Shea was hoping you might have found her and brought her home."

Calvin responded for Katherine as he helped her out of the room and down the steps. On their trip down the staircase they passed other agents running up. When they stepped across the door leading outside, Katherine was engulfed by her husband and sons, who pushed passed the protective arms of the multitude of British agents as well as local Irish police.

Katherine pulled back from her husband's embrace.

"Thomas there was an evil woman. She murdered Keller and now she has Ashley."

Agent Gibson put his arms around them both and directed them to start walking toward the house.

"Please try not to worry. We will get your daughter back. Let us collect ourselves over a spot of sherry. It will settle our nerves. Katherine, I need your help along with the one who tends your sheep. By the way, its Calvin right. Where the devil is he?"

The party stopped for a moment to quickly scan the landscape of humanity. Gibson ordered one of the passing agents to find Calvin and direct him to join them at the house immediately. Thomas looked at Katherine as if to say "good luck!"

"Was it money they were after?"

"No! You're not going to believe this, Thomas. She is after the tears of Mary."

In unison, the father and the three sons responded, "The tears of Mary!"

"So this woman is a lunatic," replied Thomas.

"She may be crazy, but Calvin's the one who told her that they were buried with Saint Patrick at Saul."

"Saul. Well that confirms where they're headed. Please excuse me. I need to make a phone call. I will catch up with you at the house in a few minutes. Once again, Mr. and Mrs. O'Shea, we will do everything in our power to get your daughter home."

CHAPTER 37:

The jet-helicopter flew at a high rate of speed about thirty feet above the sea. The turquoise water whisked past the window at a hypnotic pace, practically putting Ashley in a trance. Her anger was beginning to change to fear, which was enhanced when Ivy reached over and snapped one end of a handcuff to her wrist and the other to the arm rest of her seat. She was wondering what Ivy had in store for her once she deemed her usefulness to be over.

The aircraft began to slow. When it did, the nose dipped, allowing Ashley to see over the pilot's heads. In the distance appeared a familiar site, an island that Ashley immediately recognized as a place she had just visited not more than two months earlier for a friend's wedding.

The Isle of Man, she thought to herself. *This 220-square-mile island sits in the middle of the Irish Sea about eighty miles from Downpatrick or Saul. This must be what Ivy meant by island hopping. But what treasure? Calvin already told her the diamonds were in Saul.* They began circling a boat anchored near the shore.

The boat appeared to be empty, but they hovered over the vessel for several seconds while Ivy talked to someone on a cell phone. Her conversation seemed as if she was unexpectedly negotiating with someone, and by the tone of her voice she was becoming very agitated.

"Oh very well. An additional five thousand pounds. So where are you?

"Swine!"

Ivy folded the phone and tossed it in the empty seat across from her.

"They are on top," she announced to the pilot as she pointed, directing him to ascend the rock face of the cliff in front of them. They flew toward the shore, where a lone dinghy sat cradled in the sand, then broke straight up over the crest of the cliff to be greeted by a lush, grassy meadow. Three hundred yards or so ahead an old truck sat parallel a gravel drive. The drive was virtually hidden by the tall timothy grass but exposed itself when the pilot buzzed over the top of the vehicle. Two men sat on the tailgate, leaning back against what appeared to be two white crates, both about three feet long by two feet wide and two feet deep. The chopper made a quick circle, then set down about thirty feet from the truck.

Ashley was facing forward and didn't have a good view of the truck and men, and she couldn't move because she was cuffed to the seat. Her quick observation before they landed was that the men on the ground were in their early to late twenties, possibly students of the local university, but they didn't strike her as being thugs or villains.

Ivy reached under her seat and pulled out a black briefcase, then followed her two men out the door, leaving Ashley with the pilot. They were only gone for a few minutes before the men returned, each carrying one of the heavy-duty plastic crates. They slid the heavy boxes on the floor directly in front of her feet. The worn stenciled word *Windscale* was written on the each of their sides. A closer inspection of the boxes revealed that they were solid and locked tight but very scuffed up. Just then Ivy appeared and crawled up into the aircraft. The pilot accelerated the engine, increasing the velocity of the blades. She gave one of her gunman a gesture and he disappeared immediately but returned a few minutes later with the briefcase in tow. He jumped in and slid the door shut. The helicopter rose to the sky, exposing Ashley to yet more needless violence, the sickening sight of two bodies sprawled out face down alongside their pickup.

"The Isle of Man. Looks to me like the isle of dead man." This was Ivy's sick and sadistic response as the helicopter flew back over the water, heading back to Ireland.

CHAPTER 38:

The events of earlier that day at the O'Shea castle and the Isle of man were history now, and most of these events were unbeknownst to the four men currently staking out Saint Patrick's grave. All that was left was for Austin and agents Kenny and Smyth, and of course Bryan, was to wait for Ivy Johnson to show—perhaps a feat easier said than done.

British agent Smyth concluded his briefing by telling Austin of his phone call from Gibson regarding the successful freeing of Katherine and Calvin earlier that afternoon. He also informed them that Ivy along with Ashley were already gone before they arrived. The anxiety in the room after Smyth finished his update raised several octaves. They were all anticipating the arrival of Ms. Johnson at any moment.

"I need to get back outside; I don't suppose you guys have a plan."

"The plan, as you refer to it, my young American chap, is to retrieve the stolen plutonium, as well as protect the diamonds.

This unfortunate situation now exclusively belongs to MI6 British intelligence. It's our rogue agent who has gone amok, it's our plutonium, and it's on our United Kingdom soil. So basically what I'm saying is that I am in charge. The English Navy has a ship in position to keep the Yemen yacht from leaving the Irish Sea if necessary. Agent Gibson, with his men, should be arriving momentarily, but keeping their distance as not to spook Ms. Johnson, keeping in mind she pretty much knows all of our routine moves. We know she will be minding all possible traps. We can not risk moving in any more agents within this immediate area. It's now one o'clock a.m. My guess is that Ivy and her band of terrorists will be arriving at any moment. So it's just the three of us against who knows how many.

"If you two stay in here and out of my way, it will be an even fight. I need to go complete my mission."

I walked across the dark room, aided only by the moonlight illuminating the room through the windows whose blinds had not been closed. He opened the door to an awaiting Irish sumo wrestler, better known as Bryan, who turned around and said, "My partner and I will take care of your rogue agent; Mr. Smyth, you and Kenny just need to watch our back.

"Before you move in, be damn sure she has the plutonium. Right now I could give a crap about any diamonds. Remember you are on assignment to me and have total obligation to follow my orders. You screw up and I will personally have your head. Got that, Seaman Brock?"

I didn't reply to Kenny. He just shut the door and looked past Bryan and down the steps.

"I'm not much happy working with a damn Brit; I'm more comfortable shooting at them."

"Right now I know exactly what you mean, Bryan. I'm not much happy, as you say, working with either one. Where is the rest of my Seal team when I need them? Bryan, I need you to go back to your car and keep watch, like we planned. Don't walk in the open. If you have to, take the long way around."

"Don't worry, boss. I won't screw up again."

We were about to walk back to resume our previous posts when I grabbed Bryan and pulled him back. They stood motionless under the overhang, flush against the wall.

"There is a helicopter coming. Quickly follow under the tree line around back of this building. Don't worry about going back to your car. I just need you to hide somewhere on the other side of this museum building. When I signal, you run in and grab your cousin—whatever happens you get her the hell away from here. Understand, Bryan?"

"Don't worry, Austin. I won't fail. I know my cousin's life depends on it."

The helicopter circled the compound with its spotlight scanning the grounds and then set down in the opening about fifty yards from the granite rock. During this time I was running from tree to tree, trying to keep myself from their direct vision by staying behind the helicopter. When it finally set down, I positioned myself in the shadows of a large shrub. As it turns out, I was pretty close to where I'd camped out originally.

The doors slid open and two hooded men in dark jumpsuits leaped out. They were brandishing automatic rifles and immediately began scoping their new perimeter.

Almost immediately my concentration was interrupted by lights momentarily illuminating the bush I was lying under. The lights turned out to belong to a small car turning into the parking lot, then speeding over to the parked pay-loader, where it skidded to a stop. The doors flew open and out jumped three more almost identically clothed and armed men. After a brief second or two, one began climbing the steps to the cab of the large piece of equipment.

I thought to myself, *So I guess this is how these guys are planning to unearth the treasure. This could begin to get very interesting.* This also got me thinking, *I hope my other three counterparts won't screw up.* But I had this uneasy feeling.

I looked back at the chopper. Still no Ivy or Ashley, but I couldn't see inside the craft. I needed to get closer. The four men on the ground now converged around the loader; they pulled out from the car trunk what seemed to be a generator with a portable floodlight and loaded it into the bucket of the machine. They fired up the loader's engine, letting it idle for a few minutes, and then lifted its six-foot-wide bucket from the ground.

This was the moment to make my move closer to the helicopter; it appeared all efforts of the bad guys were focused on moving the giant pay-loader from the parking lot to the grave.

I put my head down and ran as hard as I could toward the now quiet aircraft. When I arrived at the rear tail, I slid myself underneath. Advancing a round into the chamber of my gun, my plan was to get the drop on whoever was left inside, figuring they were also focused on the happenings outside the now right side of the helicopter, and so I would make my surprise entry via the left side.

Saying a quick prayer first, I rolled myself left until I was clear of the fuselage, then vaulted straight up with my weapon poised. To my surprise I was two minutes too late. Ivy and Ashley were exiting the right side simultaneously as I rolled, so I was now pointing my gun through the empty cabin toward the back of their heads as they walked away.

Luckily, the pilot was also looking out the starboard side and didn't witness my mistimed ambush. I immediately ducked back down, but not before noticing the two white PVC containers on the floor with what looked to be worn government markings stenciled on the sides. I presumed the two containers housed the plutonium as Smyth predicted. Crawling back under the helicopter, I watched Ivy drag Ashley by the arm in the direction of the rock. Ashley's hands were cuffed behind her. This sent a shiver of rage up my spine. I could barley contain myself. I wanted to go out, guns a-blazing, and get my girl back, but I knew I must remain focused and not let my personal feelings cloud my judgments or I might end up getting her killed.

Ivy's men worked very expediently unloading the generator and setting up the floodlights. They were aware of the limited time before they were discovered. At all times two of Ivy's men were on watch, their rifles fully extended and ready to fire.

Ivy immediately assumed her role as commander while orchestrating the excavation. She was constantly on watch. They fired up the generator and light next to the granite rock, which lit up the area, rivaling an operating room at a hospital. During this activity something caught Ivy's eye on the second floor of the museum. I remember thinking to myself, *She must have spotted those two bozos in the window.* Suddenly she turned away and said something in Arabic that sent one of her gunman running in the direction of Smyth and Kenny.

I had to get myself out from under the chopper now. If Ivy was able to spot something from up on the second floor of a building several yards away, it was only a matter of time before she would see me too. My first thought was that I should take out the pilot. This would ground them. However, I decided it was too soon, and he didn't appear to be armed, so he wasn't a threat. I crawled out the back and down to a tombstone about twenty feet away. I would wait here until the right moment presented itself. Then I would make my move.

Ivy became increasingly interested in what was going on with her sentry. She kept trying to communicate via her radio while looking up toward the museum, but it was apparent she wasn't making contact. She finally became so frustrated she ripped her ear- and mouthpiece out and threw it on the ground. Sensing something might have been wrong, she screamed at her men, which immediately motivated them to pick up the pace. She waved the operator on the loader closer to the rock; he lowered the giant bucket and crept forward till the flat steel of the bucket introduced itself to the granite, causing a spark. The wheels spun as the engine revved. The iron beast belched out black smoke as it fought the granite bulwark for its position. Finally the rock gave way, it moved back about six feet. Ivy waved off the loader operator. He put the beast in reverse and backed up several feet away, then shut the machine down.

Oh what a pathetic sight of human behavior this was: defiling of a sacred yet humble monument of a saint no less. I wanted to throw up or cry, or both.

This act of vile greed rivaled anything that I could have ever imagined. I knew it was only a matter of time before these animals would get what was coming to them, and the real punishment yet to be given wasn't to be doled out here on Earth.

Enough is enough, even though Ivy still had a hold of Ashley's arm. She stood about two feet away; plenty of room for me to get off a clean shot. I stood up slowly, extended my nine millimeter, and rested my arm on the top of the tombstone. I inhaled a breath, then slowly let it out as I tightened my grip and began to squeeze my finger.

Pop! Pop!

Dirt flew and bodies scattered. One of Ivy's men fell lifeless to the ground. Yet the shots fired did not come from my gun. From around the side of the building came Smyth and Kenny. Their government-issued pistols were drawn and pointed. I heard Smyth announce to Ivy, "Agent Johnson, surrender your weapons!" She ignored his request. Instead she took quick aim and shot Smyth, hitting him in the thigh, collapsing him to the ground. This immediately set off a barrage of gunfire. Kenny miraculously wasn't hit; he grabbed Smyth by the back of his collar and dragged him behind a large grave marker, returning fire as he went. By now all her men were aimlessly firing at anything that moved.

From out behind my makeshift bunker, I ran toward the crowd. My first shot hit the operator of the loader between the eyes. Everything from this point forward was basically instinctive and reactionary. I took aim at Ivy, but her sporadic movements dictated my instantaneous decision not to shoot for fear of hitting Ashley. By now I had completely drawn all the fire away from Kenny and Smyth, and it was now directed towards me. Things were moving very fast but at the same time it almost seamed as if I was in slow motion. I heard Ashley cry out my name as I dove through the air, firing my weapon in the general direction of one of the enemy and hitting the closest gunman, tackling him before he got off his shot. My momentum took us both off our feet and over the edge of the newly formed excavation, tumbling down through the hole, ending our flight in what appeared to be an exposed sarcophagus. I was now on top of Habib and lying next to the remains of Saint Patrick. This was my low point. I had just violated a religious shrine by taking out this dirt bag. I was upset to say the least. So as a result of my frustration I rendered a forearm shiver to this creep that sent him immediately to sleep.

The rapping of automatic weapons suddenly ceased above me. I rolled over and looked up at the wicked witch, Johnson, holding her gun up to Ashley's temple.

"I mean it, sailor boy. I have nothing to lose. You and the others stop with your heroics or I will splatter her brains all over this worthless Irish dirt."

I stood up and stepped aside the moaning terrorist coming to at my feet.

"Throw out your weapon, and come up here, and tell your American comrade over there to do the same."

I tossed my gun up as requested and crawled out of the hole. I was now standing face to face with Ivy. Ashley lunged forward. Her forehead brushed my chest momentarily, but before I could embrace her she was yanked back.

"Let her go!"

"I will let her go when you call off the others; otherwise in a few seconds you'll be wearing her all over your shirt."

"They don't take orders from me. You know that, Johnson. Those two over there could care less if you shoot us. In fact they don't give a damn about the diamonds; all they are interested in is the crates of plutonium you have got on the floor of that helicopter."

Ivy hesitated, thinking over her next move. She looked at me and then over at Kenny, now poised behind the tombstone with his arm erect and his gun ready to shoot.

"You know he is right. If it comes down to us or the plutonium, he will be the one shooting me in my head."

I thought to myself, *I'm just bluffing. but I am pretty sure Kenny would really do that.*

"Listen, Johnson, I don't give a damn about the diamonds or the plutonium; I just want you to leave the girl and get the hell out of here. I will even help you load the diamonds on the chopper."

I jumped back down in the hole before Ivy could make her final decision. I felt that I was out of options and our lives were worth a hell of a lot more than any bag of diamonds. And as far as the plutonium was concerned, I had total confidence that either the British Navy or my U.S. Navy would blow her chopper or the yacht into a million pieces if they wanted to.

Habib was still moving around inside the newly exposed six-by-four sarcophagus beneath where the granite rock once lay, but he jumped to life when Ivy yelled something to him in Arabic.

The cobwebs were beginning to clear from the startled hired killer's pea brain, and he began to focus on his new surroundings. Near his feet, beside what appeared to be the linen-wrapped remains of a body, a three-foot-tall pot appeared though the shadows.

The grave's appearance looked to be that of a pauper instead of what one would imagine the final resting place of a saint to look like. The rugged clay pot was the only resemblance to any treasure one could make out with the dark dusty conditions.

Ivy seamed to accept my offer. She didn't shoot me when I jumped back down in the hole, probably because she knew if she took her gun off of Ashley for an instant Kenny would take her out, and she couldn't rely on her two remaining gunman to take out Kenny.

Ivy's army was down to two men above ground whose duties were to keep watch, train their weapons on and fend off Kenny and Smyth, and at the same time assist Habib in the hole. The evening of the odds did not seem to detract her from her goal, which was to obtain the mythical gems.

I stood and stared at the surroundings, waiting for Habib to do something, and then Ivy screeched out another order in Arabic.

Habib took a step forward and leaned over and clutched the ancient clay container with one hand and with the other pulled out the four-inch diameter wax and cork plug that sealed the vessel.

A huge fireball of brilliant light burst through the not-yet-fully-opened jar. It looked like a bolt of lightning shot out, hitting Habib in the head, knocking him back off his feet again. The intense glow remained, totally engulfing the tomb and cocooning around a screaming Muslim who seemed as if he were being electrocuted.

I took my foot and gently placed it on top of the jar, pushing the plug back down, sealing the opening. The brilliant light show stopped. I looked down at a hysterical Habib, now completely white. His once jet-black hair was now as white as the sand of the Sierra.

"Bring me the jar, Austin!" demanded Ivy from atop the earthen bank.

I picked up the clay jar as ordered and handed it up to one of the awaiting gunman. There was no way I was leaving this pathetic babbling swine lying any longer next to the holy remains of Saint Patrick, so I grabbed him by the collar and pulled his sorry, crying limp body out of the hole with me.

There was a sudden realization that my life might soon be over. I was now standing a few feet away from Ivy and a terrified Ashley, a clear shot from either one of Ivy's gunman.

They had what they came for and if Ivy could make it back to the awaiting helicopter she could expend either gunman and of course me. I also knew that Kenny was about ready to initiate an attack. There was no way he would let Ivy board that aircraft.

What I needed was a diversion, and God must have been listening.

Boom! A huge explosion shook the ground, practically shaking us all off our feet. The car three of the terrorists drove, which was parked in the lot, exploded, lifting it in the air five or six feet before it crashed back to earth in a ball of fire. Running through the smoke, shotgun a-blazing, was Bryan to the rescue.

This immediately set off a chain of events. Bryan did not hit anything with his shotgun; however, his plastic explosives he planted underneath the car caused just the diversion I was looking for.

Ivy immediately reached down and picked up the heavy urn while still not relinquishing her grip on Ashley. I kicked the gun out of her hand, disarming her for the moment; however, my concern was now focused on the two gunmen who were firing at Bryan, who was running full force toward them. Bryan took a round in the arm, but that didn't seem to slow his advance, but I knew he was in trouble; he apparently was out of ammunition, because he threw his gun down but kept running.

I reached down and picked up Ivy's gun that I kicked from her hands and dropped one gunman, almost instantaneously. The second gunman dropped as well, this one a victim of Kenny's marksmanship.

Looking up I noticed the calvary arriving, three or four black Mercedes kicking up a cloud of dust were converging their way from the street to the parking lot. Their timing was about six minutes too late, thanks to Bryan's fireworks, complements of his Irish Republican Army days.

CHAPTER 39:

The noise of the chopper blades and the whine of the jet engine gave my heart an immediate sinking feeling. I quickly turned around to see Ivy running to the helicopter with the clay pot under one arm and dragging along her hostage with the other.

"Austin!" Ashley cried out.

Ivy had replaced her gun with a knife, which she had now under Ashley's throat as she used her as a shield until she made her way to the aircraft.

The pilot was becoming very anxious for obvious reasons; Ivy no more than rolled the jar onto the floor when the bird began to take off. Ivy climbed on, leaving the still cuffed Ashley to fend for herself as bullets zinged by their heads, hitting the fuselage. The rounds were coming from the direction of the newly arrived agents; both Bryan and I began screaming intensely at the shooters. The wild flying lead was not the only danger now facing Ashley; she was now dangling about six feet in the air. Her cuffs were hooked on the landing rail of the helicopter, preventing her from entering the cabin.

I was running at full speed as I jumped up on a grave marker, which gave me enough lift that I just was able to grab the same rail Ashley was clinging to.

I pulled myself up, locking my arm over the runner as I swung my leg over. The chopper wildly flew from side to side; either the pilot was trying to be evasive to escape the trailing barrage of bullets, or he was trying to knock us off, or most likely both.

The chopper was now well out of range of any flying lead, but I had no idea how high we were or how fast we were traveling. The full moon that earlier lit up the landscape was now clouded over, and the only illumination we got was from the lights on the helicopter itself, which wasn't much.

In front of me was a terrified girl hanging on for dear life. I slid myself forward on the rails, inch by inch until I reached her.

She was understandably as white as a ghost. The chain on her cuffs was lodged between the rail runner and the support bar, and to complicate things further her hands were still cuffed together. I looked up and the sliding door to the cabin was shut. That bitch left her out here anticipating she would fall off. I knew once I broke her free I would have a hard time convincing her to release her tight grip, allowing her to crawl up and then inside.

"Ashley, honey, I'm here, and we're going to be all right!"

I was able to free her chain, but there was no way she would be able to negotiate the climb while her hands were cuffed.

I reached up and grabbed the latch to the door. It was locked. So with my other hand I pulled the pistol, which I acquired earlier, and pointed it at the door. After I leaned over and warned Ashley, I shot a hole through the locked latch and slid the door open.

Ivy greeted me with a snap kick that grazed my shoulder, but I caught her foot and pushed her back. She fell against the far side wall and then slid down to the floor.

"Give me keys to the cuffs now!" I yelled as I pointed the gun toward her, still standing on the landing rail, halfway in and halfway out.

"Go ahead and shoot then. You still won't have the keys."

Ivy pulled out the keys and opened the window next to her head; she dangled them as if she was going to toss them.

I turned the gun in the direction of the pilot.

"You're not crazy enough to shoot the pilot, are you? That won't get your keys either. Ha!"

I was that crazy, more like desperate. The shot hit the pilot in the lower leg. My aim was right above the ankle. For a moment I thought I really screwed up. The chopper pitched and rolled severely from side to side. I hung onto the crossbars with one arm and onto Ashley with the other. The pilot was screaming in pain and cussing at me in Arabic; however, he finally got the aircraft back under control.

"Listen, you drop those keys out the window or you get the next bullet between the eyes. We either all land safely or none of us at all!"

I must have gotten her attention by shooting the pilot. Ivy lowered the keys to the floor and slid them my direction, and with an extended reach I was able to grab them. I stuffed the gun back down my pants and lowered myself on top of Ashley, stabilizing myself against the fuselage.

Miraculously I was able to get the cuffs off quickly, but now came the hard part: talking Ashley into trusting me with her life and letting go long enough to rise up and into the helicopter.

Ashley is a tougher girl than I gave her credit for. Immediately after I un-cuffed her and with a little coaxing she was ready to let go. I guided her right hand up over her head till she was able to reach and hold a handle above the step into the cabin. Then I scooted myself back and off of her and slowly stood up. Ashley's head was facing aft, or toward the tail of the helicopter, which meant her butt was facing the direction of travel and into the wind. So the wind blew her long auburn hair up over her head and covered her eyes, which also made it more difficult.

"On the count of three we're going to do this. Ashley, you just need to pull yourself up. Don't worry. I will grab you as soon as you do. When I have you, you let go of the handle; we will roll right into the aircraft. Do you understand?"

She nodded.

"One, two, three—now, honey!"

Ashley did exactly as I instructed; however, as she moved her legs up underneath her and started to lift up, her foot slipped off the runner. She let out a terrified scream as she began to fall. I caught her wrist and with one arm I pulled her one-hundred-pound frame up within my clutches. Then with her torso tightly squeezed in my grasp, I rolled us into the cabin.

I could feel Ashley's heart pounding rapidly as she was lying on top of me. Her face was pressed into my chest, and her hair draped over both of us. I was waiting days to have this girl back in my arms, and for a few seconds I was in heaven, but the sound of clapping hands brought me quickly back to Earth—more correctly about fifty feet above Earth.

"How wonderful. The hero saves the damsel in distress. You two are pathetic; I should have shot you both when I had the chance."

As soon as I heard Ivy's evil voice, I reached for the gun I had stuffed in the back of my pants, but it was gone. It must have dropped out when I was out on the rail.

"I guess I can't convince you to turn this bird around without shooting you first."

"With what might you shoot me with, old chap. I watched your—I mean my—pistol exit your trousers the moment you and your little girl friend came rolling through the door. By the way, I must say, good form.

"No, I am afraid you are now accompanying me on this journey until we land at my destination or my pilot blacks out and we crash."

"Well it looks like I'm up for a cruise on a luxury yacht then."

"Oh you'll get your cruise all right; I see that Smyth fell for my decoy. This is exactly what infuriates me about Mi-6; they have an endless list of morons like Smyth and Gibson, which they are willing to promote on a daily basis. But show a little aggression, a little ambition, a little more intelligence than their superiors'…well, what do they do? They sweep you under the rug to be later thrown out with the rubbish.

"Do they actually think that I am stupid enough to use a conspicuous thirty-five-meter yacht anchored for days right under their noses as my getaway vehicle?

"Well British so-called intelligence will be talking about Agent Ivy Johnson for years to come after this. They will say 'Johnson; she's the agent that MI 6 let slip away, a dreadful day for England.'"

As soon as Ivy stopped ranting, Ashley and I looked at each other, astonished. It was apparent that what motivated this crazed woman was rage toward her previous employer, British Intelligence. This was all about revenge for Ivy; she was driven by the opportunity to become infamous at the expense of MI-6 and even the CIA. In her twisted mind her acclaim would be being known as a notorious mastermind; however, what she really will be immortalized as is a murderous traitor and terrorist.

The helicopter took a severe dip; the pilot was indeed struggling and might have been blacking out.

"You might want to attend to your pilot, Johnson; his crashing will ruin your chance at becoming immortal."

"I will see to him, Austin. That witch is incapable of rendering aid to anyone."

Ashley got up and walked to the ailing pilot, but when she got next to him and knelt down to inspect his wound, the man snapped at her and pushed her away.

"Unable to help the pilot, Florence Nightingale?" snarled Ivy.

"Well, Austin, my quick observation is that it looks like the wound has stopped bleeding; I think he will be able to get where we need to go."

On Ashley's return to her seat, she nearly tripped over one of the crates of plutonium that contributed to the crowded floor, which had little spare space. Accompanying the crates of course was the supposed humble clay jar housing the diamonds of Mary Magdalene.

With Ashley at my side and Ivy sitting across the way, we were all now silent and staring at the display at our feet. *I cannot believe that I am within an arm's length of something as sacred and as meaningful as this shrine.* The ironic thing was that this hallowed clay receptacle, which represented love and eternal life, was sitting next to a receptacle that housed a metallic element capable of the death and destruction of thousands or even millions of lives. Good and evil, everlasting life or eternal damnation: Before us were perhaps the ultimate symbols of heaven and hell. *Wow,* I thought to myself, *this is way too deep philosophic thought for this Indiana boy.*

"So, Ivy, how do you explain what happened back at the grave when your man pulled the plug out of that jar? The story must be true that the diamonds that lie within this jar, can only be viewed and enjoyed by the pure at heart. I guess old Habib wasn't that pure, was he? What are you going do to when your Saudi client wants you to show him the diamonds?"

"I will unplug the pot and dump them out before his eyes to see. You see, Mr. Brock, I don't buy any of this mumbo jumbo of the diamonds mystically turning into water or that they shoot out electricity or whatever. I'm sure there is a perfectly good scientific explanation of what occurred."

"Okay then. Go ahead and open the vase now."

"I don't play games, and I don't need to prove anything. especially to you."

I heard the pilot talking and looked up to see him on the radio, and then Ivy chimed in, continuing to converse with him in his own tongue. Something was about to happen. My guess was we were about to land, but it was still too dark to see out the windows, and there was no sign of lights.

CHAPTER 40:

The clouds were parting somewhat, and the moonlight began to expose the water below us. This at least answered the question of whether we were over land or sea. I wish I knew our coordinates, and if I did I wish I could relay them back to Kenny. It suddenly hit me, my small satellite phone; it was still in my hip pocket. If it had enough charge left I could hit the auto-dial and maybe they could track it.

I felt the chopper begin to bank; Ashley and I were now able to see what appeared to be a large trawler, maybe eighty feet long. We buzzed over the bridge, and then I could tell that this was not an ordinary fishing vessel. There weren't any outriggers, but it did have a landing pad, which lit up as we passed overhead.

I told Ashley to brace herself. I wasn't sure how rough our landing might be due to the condition I put the pilot in. We hovered directly over the vessel for about thirty seconds before slowly descending. Thank God the winds were light. I could tell he was struggling, trying to use his bum foot.

I yelled over to Ivy, "Tell the pilot that one of us could help so he doesn't have to use his bad foot."

"I'm not telling him anything. Do you honestly think he would accept help from the man who just shot him a little more than an hour earlier. He'll get us down."

The tone of her voice wasn't overly convincing; however, he made the landing. We landed a little hard, but nevertheless we touched down and were now on board the ship.

The pilot immediately killed the engine, and within seconds both side doors slid open and there our welcoming committee awaited, and they weren't exactly Hula girls doling out flowered leis and beaded necklaces.

Here were more Middle Eastern armed men, only this group wasn't dressed in matching fatigues. In fact, some were barely dressed at all, only wearing dingy boxer shorts, but they were all dirty and they were all unshaved. But the worse thing was their body odor. Obviously hygiene wasn't a priority on this ship and this bunch smelled like they had been on a long voyage.

I felt like we were a display at a museum. Both door openings left and right were crammed full of heads. Half the men were staring at the white crates and clay jar on the floor, and the other half of the men were staring at Ashley.

Ivy wasn't amused at all the attention. She screamed at the men and made hand gestures trying to back them up, but her wishes went disobeyed until a commanding voice from behind parted the crowd.

A tall bearded man approached the starboard door and peered in.

"So what took you so long, Ms. Johnson?" Clearly the captain of this ship was obviously bilingual. This man didn't mince words.

Who are these people, and why is my pilot slumped over? You promised me there would be no trouble. I am not paid well enough to deal with trouble. I was only hired to deliver you and your cargo to Haifa.

"There is no trouble, only a minor setback. I assure you that I have everything under control. This American shot your pilot, but he is now weaponless, and the girl is basically harmless. You may do as you wish with them; I assure you that everything will be fine."

"Very well, but if everything is not as you say, I will personally shoot you in the head and cut you up for bait. As far as your stowaways, they are your responsibility, not mine. You deal with them."

The captain turned around and grabbed a pistol from the belt of one of his subordinates, then tossed it to Ivy.

"Don't shoot them until we get in international waters, I will inform you when that happens."

Those were pleasant words to hear before the captain departed.

I took Ashley's hand as we stood up, moving her intentionally between Ivy and myself, shielding me from view. I pulled the phone out of my hip pocket and hit the auto-send button, then tossed it underneath the seat. I could only hope that it would send out a traceable signal and that Kenny or King would be waiting to receive it. I had no idea where we were, other than in the middle of an ocean. There was no way I could speak on the phone without getting caught. Also it was highly likely that I would be searched, so leaving the functioning phone in the chopper seamed to be my best option.

Ivy, having a gun now, really had little effect on us; she was preoccupied with her new treasures and paid little attention to our actions. The reality was that we were not an immediate threat by being miles offshore somewhere in the Irish or Celtic Sea, possibly even as far the North Atlantic, on a vessel with twenty or thirty armed mercenaries. Even though it wasn't as if the odds were stacked in our favor to take over their boat, we still were the main focus of the curious crew.

So Ashley and I sat on a crate on the forward deck and watched Ivy supervise the unloading of her stolen merchandise with the glow of the morning sun beginning to appear over the horizon.

Ivy was able to commandeer a couple of the crew to help with the heavy lifting, especially the white crates of plutonium, which they brought over and set next to us. Ironically, when they were done, Ivy sat down next to us. She appeared to be relieved and exalted at the same time. There was no exchange of conversation—not even momentary eye contact. She pulled herself up on the crate in the sitting position, then laid down flat on her back, staring up at the sky. Finally she spoke.

"You know, Austin, we really are not that different, you and I. Very skilled and dedicated and devoted to a cause. It took me several years to realize that the cause that I was devoted to wasn't worthy of my efforts. We are merely slaves, investing long hours of sweat and blood, and for what? Do you realize that as I speak Saddam Hussein of Iraq is trying to outbid the Yemen for this weapon-grade plutonium? Their offer now is one hundred million dollars, and a Saudi wants to pay me fifty million for the diamonds. What cause is better risking my life for than me? If I were killed a year ago, do you think the British would give a damn. They would just replace me with some other poor sap the next day and business would go on?"

Ivy was just talking; she wasn't necessarily talking to us. She didn't wait for a response. When she finished she jumped down from the crate and walked away. It was just as well. What I had to tell her I know she did not want to hear.

We were off and steaming full speed ahead, the recurring thought I kept having was, *Is Ivy going to try to execute us or not once we get into international waters? Whatever, I need to have a plan just in case.*

A few minutes went by and Ivy returned, this time with her satellite phone stuck in her ear and talking again in Arabic.

"So, Johnson, I assume the captain and his men have no idea what your contraband is? I guess that's a stupid question, isn't it? If they only knew what they had aboard their ship. Probably not much honor among thieves is there, Johnson? Do you suppose they subscribe to your philosophy of being devoted to their own cause and not yours? I'm thinking total anarchy would occur; how about you?"

"Cut the crap, and to think I was beginning to like you, Austin. Are you threatening me? Look at all these men around you; none of them can understand any of the queen's English except for the captain, and he would just as soon shoot you than listen to anything that comes out of your mouth. So I don't know how anyone would pass on our little secret, do you, Mr. Brock?

"You know, your shooting the pilot could actually have turned out a lot worse for me. Apparently he only has a fractured bone. They splinted him up and he will be ready to fly me out of here. That's the good news. The bad news is he wants to get revenge. He's indicated he would like to shoot you in the ankle as well before he leaves. I told him I would consider it. By the way, I wasn't really planning on going all the way to Haifa with these stinking bastards. Always keeping one step ahead. That's the key, Austin.

"I have chosen to sell the plutonium to Mr. Hussein; his people are working on making the wire transfer to my Cayman account as we speak."

Just then a man appeared from the shadows of the companionway. The three of us stared at him as he approached us. The man dressed and appeared different then any of the other crew. He was carrying a silver case, which he laid next to Ivy.

"Verification. You didn't expect anyone would pay me for my merchandise sight-unseen, did you? Dr Yarmar here was selected and hired jointly by my two bidders to verify the plutonium and also discretely escort it through Israeli Customs, then trek it over land, in this case to Baghdad. The doctor here can conduct a radiation test without opening the lead-lined boxes. When it is complete and he is confident of his findings, he will call my client back and they will complete the transfer of funds.

"What about the diamonds?"

"I'm afraid the diamonds must come with me; they are a girl's best friend, you know."

Dr Yarmar opened his case and pulled out what appeared to be some sort of complicated Geiger counter devise, which he placed on top of one the crates. I just realized the crates the doctor was beginning to work on at our feet might potentially be giving off small amounts of radiation, so I grabbed Ashley and we jumped off our wooden perch.

Some of the crew was refueling the helicopter and dragging a camouflage tarp over it, other crew members were extending the outriggers—I assume to make it appear that this ship was nothing more than a large fishing vessel.

We pretty much roamed the boat as we pleased the rest of the day; Ashley was always at my side. They gave us food and water in the galley and we freshened up the best we could at the filthy heads.

I was sure we had made it to international waters by now, and it'd been at least a couple of hours since we had crossed paths with Ms. Johnson. So hopefully shooting us was not on her agenda. Perhaps she was just waiting for the pilot to do her dirty work.

CHAPTER 41:

The day was long and very uneasy for us; it was as if we were on death row and awaiting either execution or a pardon from the governor. I played down the threats to Ashley. Worrying her more than she was already worried had no benefit. It was hard for me to get a handle on what our fate would be. We were helplessly at the mercy of Ivy or the captain, and for that matter maybe the pilot. Jumping over the side was not an option and there was no way we could untie a life raft without being noticed, unless there was some sort of diversion. So I kept a lookout for an opportunity to present itself and or a diversion to happen, in case the lifeboat thing might be our only escape. Who knows. Maybe they will take mercy on us and cast us off anyway.

The late afternoon found us sitting on a bench, leaning back against the exterior cabin wall, gazing to the west. I was silently hoping we were not looking at our final sunset. There were enough saps with weapons dangling from their sides or around their necks that I was confident I would be able to take one away and at least go out with a fight. They always said in the Seals, "In a fight, if you think that you're not going to make it, at least make a hell of a show."

Suddenly our peaceful sunset was interrupted by two crewmen sporting shotguns. They were there to escort us back to the front of the ship.

When we rounded the side of the boat I could tell this wasn't good. Ivy and the crutch-toting pilot, plus three other observers including Dr Yarmar, were all standing in a half circle. They were anxiously awaiting our arrival. This scene had a funny familiarity to it—well, at least to me. The thought that rushed through my mind was from an old movie where Christians were being led into the coliseum by the Romans to be eaten by the lions.

"Ms. O'Shea and Mr. Brock, I thought you would like to see me off. My work here is complete. The good doctor has confirmed to the Iraq dictator's scientist that the plutonium was of pure grade, and I have just verified through my Cayman banker that I am a very rich woman.

"Well, as I told you earlier, it seems as if the pilot here wants to satisfy a little revenge before he flies us to France. I tried to persuade him to turn the other cheek, but he would have none of that."

I walked over to the pilot and stood toe to toe with him, staring down at his grubby little face. Sweat beads began to form on his forehead, and his arm, hanging to his side, which gripped a pistol, began to tremble. I wasn't a bully by nature, but I'd be damned if I was going to just let this little worm shoot me. My adrenalin was pushing my bravado to the max, so I continued to play up my best John Wayne.

The surrounding crowd was chanting in a foreign dialect, but I was sure they were not rooting for me. I wasn't about to take my eyes off of him for a second, or surely he would make his move.

"Hey, Johnson, why don't you ask this little fly where he wants me to shoot him next, once I take his gun away?"

I no more than got that out of my mouth, when I heard "Look out, Austin."

Ashley's warning wasn't in time for me to stop the butt of a rifle to my lower back that brought me to my knees. As I was falling, things seemed to be in slow motion. I couldn't help but notice a grin forming on the pilot's face as he raised his gun to fire. But his gun wasn't pointed at my foot; he had no intent on just wounding me, judging from the barrel now within inches of my head. He planned on executing me.

"Hey look over here, you bitch! Look who's got your diamonds. Let's show everyone how beautiful they are."

Ashley was dragging the heavy jar across the deck, screaming at the top of her lungs. She immediately drew the attention of the hysterical crowd, which included of course Ivy, who had left her treasure unattended to take part in the vigilant ritual.

"Stop right there. Get away from that now!"

Ivy drew her hand gun and shot a warning shot into the air. "The next one hits you between the eyes."

Ashley momentarily stopped, so the crowd turned back around to focus on the main event, the "execution," but not for long.

"Hey check this out," screamed Ashley.

Ashley had a grip on the woven rope handle attached to the wax plug securely lodged down of the throat of the jar.

In one motion Ivy raised her arm and fired.

What happened within the next few seconds seemed to last an eternity. It was as if the events were transpiring in slow motion. I could tell what Ashley was trying to do, and I knew she was flirting with death by tormenting the devil.

As Ivy squeezed the trigger, Ashley simultaneously pulled out the plug. It was if we were standing in downtown Hong Kong on Chinese New Year. Beams of light that resembled Roman candles flew out of the jar like bees from a disturbed hive. I jumped to my feet, hitting the pilot, sending him and his gun flying through the air. The entire front half of the small ship was a glow of brilliant light. I was in survival mode. My first reaction was to get to Ashley. The beams of light shooting from the jar were hitting the assembly of men in their heads and chests, knocking them to the ground, sending them into convulsions.

Ashley was standing motionless. Tears were streaming down her face. She was mumbling, "Mary please forgive us." I threw my arms around her as we fell to the deck. As we were falling, Ashley's foot caught the jar, bringing it tumbling with us. The surge of motion sent the contents spilling out of the urn and onto the floor at our feet. Diamonds. There must have been hundreds of diamonds; their unexplainable beauty was beyond belief. A drift of shimmering radiance unseen for centuries, and only then seen by a few, lay before Ashley and me, but before our minds could register this phenomenon, the brilliant mound of diamonds faded, as did the glow of the ship. Left behind was a pool of water and a soaked scarf.

I felt the boat shift in motion as if it went from steaming to idling. Ashley was still dazed, continuing to mumble to herself, but she awakened from her trance when I gently brushed away her tears and gave her a kiss on her cheek.

In two or three minutes in our little world on this boat, we experienced Armageddon. I stood up and pulled Ashley to her feet, scattered across the deck were six moaning or crying crewman and one dead scientist, shot through the chest, apparently by the bullet intended for Ashley. The crewmen were all blinded. They had no pupils left and their hair was pure white. Standing alone and staring out to sea, Ivy looked like a statue; she was bright white from head to foot. I can only assume she was blind as well.

During the confusion I didn't notice that we had been joined by the captain and four other crewmen. Apparently they had been in the pilothouse and below deck and missed the episode.

Angry and frightened, the captain paced back and forth from port to starboard with his rifle at his ready, stopping momentarily at each one of his pathetic crewman rolled up in fetal positions on the floor. The captain became angrier with each man he attempted to interrogate; he was learning nothing from their incoherent babble.

I knew that it was only a matter of time before he would vent his frustrations, and with us being unwanted guests, I was certain we would receive the blame for the situation of his crew.

It was time to make our escape. I grabbed Ashley's arm as we started toward the back of the ship to the lifeboat. Ashley started with me, then broke away; she wasn't leaving without the tears of Mary.

"Ashley, leave it." My words went unheeded, and before I could grasp her she was out of my reach. One of the unaffected crew members noticed Ashley running back for the jar, so he pursued, but he didn't notice me in time. I reached over his shoulder and pulled his rifle away, and then with the wooded butt I administered a sleeping pill to the head of the surprised seaman. Turning, I anticipated I would find the captain and entire crew breathing down my neck, but instead they were focused on Ivy dragging one of the heavy crates of plutonium across the deck to the side rail, then heaving it up and over the side, falling to the abyss.

I stood over Ashley, guarding her as she mopped up the pooled liquid with what I assumed to be the holy saint's scarf. Across the way, Ivy looked like a zombie. Now walking over to the second crate, she appeared to be blind like the others but was navigating perfectly; also she was handling the hundred-pound lead crates with relative ease. Walking beside her, the captain was yelling at the top of his lungs, but there was no response.

She kept to her business at hand, which was dragging the second crate across the deck to the railing.

Ashley too went on completing her own task, undaunted by the other events taking place. She lovingly placed the soaked linen scarf down into the clay jar, then sealed it with the plug.

"What happened to my men, and why are you dumping your contraband over the side? What is going on? I demand you answer me now!"

The captain was becoming quite irate. His questions for Ivy where going unanswered. She wasn't responding to him in any form.

Ivy hoisted the crate onto the railing and then began to climb up alongside it. The captain reached out to grab her when a yelp from another crewman stopped his advance. For a moment all heads turned our direction. We were spotted.

From across the boat I could see the outrage in his eyes; I was now holding a gun—not just a gun, one of his guns, from one of his crew members lying on the deck. In the captain's mind that was enough evidence to blame me for the condition of his crew.

The captain advanced a round into his chamber as behind him Ivy made her suicidal leap from the railing, clutching the handles of the heavy crate as if she were clinching the reins of a silver steed, riding off to meet her maker.

I didn't wait for the splash; neither did the captain,. He sprayed the air in our direction with lead as we dove behind some stacked wooden boxes. Poking my gun from around the corner of the box, I quickly returned the favor.

Bullets were flying everywhere, and the noise was deafening. Obviously the captain wasn't concerned about putting holes in his vessel. Beside me, Ashley huddled. Wood splinters from the bullets witling away at the boxes decorated her hair; she securely embraced the clay jar as if it was providing her with some security. The gunfire intensified. I was unable to return any fire and it was apparent that our hosts were not interested in taking hostages.

Our backs were against the ever shrinking protection of the wooden boxes. I felt like we were Butch Cassidy and the Sundance Kid and we had just exhausted all of our options.

Suddenly, like a rocket being launched from a pad at Cape Canaveral about thirty meters or so off beam, the bow of a nuclear sub exploded through the surface of the water, then exposing its belly like a breaching blue whale, it plunged back into the awaiting sea.

"United States Navy," I said, the most beautiful three words of my vocabulary. "Honey, the good guys have just arrived!"

Over our shoulders and behind us the gunfire momentarily ceased. The dramatic arrival of this Seawolf class submarine had to cause these Islamic fanatics thugs to swallow hard.

I alerted Ashley to be ready to move and also to hold on; the wakes of the emerged warship would hit us hard, especially now that the power was cut on our boat.

One would think that this was all over, but apparently the captain for either the lack of brains or the accolades of becoming a martyr, decided to step up the fight.

From somewhere behind us came the deafening sound of a .50-caliber machinegun, but no sooner than the initial lead flew over our heads, the waves hit. This large converted trawler was no match for the violent waves when they hit. The boat rocked and pitched. Spray from the waves came crashing over the sides, soaking Ashley and me. During this siege from the sea, anyone standing or not bracing themselves was surely knocked off their feet, including the operator of the large-caliber gun.

Instantly, after the shock hit and before the enemy could regain its bearings, I raised up from behind our meager wooden fortress, firing my newly borrowed rifle with the objective of taking out as many bad guys as possible. To my delight, as I started to pan the ship for targets, I spotted three or four incoming black six-inch diameter spheres landing on the deck. I immediately recognized this calling card. There was a Seal unit about to board and they had just tossed up stun grenades to announce their arrival. I hit the deck momentarily, then jumped up to see grappling hooks being flailed over the side rails. The crewman on the large machinegun was the first to regain his composure and spun his gun 180 degrees to await the frogmen as they scaled the side. I took aim and removed him from contention just as the first Seal popped his head over the rail.

The smoke was thick from the grenades, and the firefight was on. I pulled Ashley up and we started toward the lifeboat, me carrying the clay container in one arm and my rifle in the other. Obviously the captain and his remaining loyal crew were no competition for this Seal unit, and it took little time for them to secure the boat; however, we were not out of danger yet. The grenades tossed earlier had started several fires, including a substantial one next to the jet fuel tank.

I set the urn down and pulled away the tarpaulin covering the lifeboat. The boat looked ragged at best but it would have to do. The billowing smoke was beginning to engulf the entire ship, choking us while we were hurriedly preparing to lower the boat. Ashley picked up the urn, placing it on board, while I was untethering the obviously never maintained lines, but as I pulled my knife out of my sheath to cut away the knotted mess, a hand grabbed my arm from behind. As a reflexive reaction I spun around to deliver a defensive blow to my attacker, but instead I was staring down the barrel of an MP-5 standard Seal-issue assault rifle.

Next came what seemed to be an eternal moment. I waited for this sailor to stand down, but instead he kept his weapon trained while his eyes scanned me from behind his standard-issue mask. Slowly the ninja-like frogman reached up and pulled off his black veil, exposing a familiar face that was grinning from ear to ear. It was my old unit leader, Chief Petty Officer Holmes.

"Nice work with the satellite phone, Father Brock. Led us right to ya."

I didn't believe my eyes. It was not only a Seal unit coming for us; it was *my Seal unit.*

Another navy comrade poked his head around the corner of the wheelhouse and yelled down the walkway to us, "The fuel tank is about to blow, its time to go!"

"Hey what's up, Austin?"

Holmes nodded toward Ashley and said, "Go save that beautiful girl. By the way, the Brits are sending a recovery vessel, so we'll catch up later." As a parting gift, Holmes slapped me on the back of my head, then exited to rejoin the rest of his pod.

I cut the rope that secured the lifeboat; the lines unreeled through the pulleys until the boat reached the water about fifteen feet below. Inside the lifeboat was a rope ladder with wood rungs, which I retained for us to use, but as I unrolled it over the side the first explosion occurred, shaking us and the boat like a ragdoll. This explosion, which turned out to be the helicopter, was much less violent than what would follow.

Ashley and I regained our balance and both glanced at the rope. Without my even telling her we didn't have time to negotiate it, she was already over the rail. Nothing was said; I just grabbed her hand and we jumped. Hell, I didn't even know if she could swim. We hit the water feet first within a few feet from the lifeboat. When we resurfaced the big explosion occurred. This sent debris flying into the air and moved the trawler, forward and sideways, causing a surge, sucking us momentarily under the water. Ashley was choking from swallowing sea water as I pulled her to the surface. Luckily we were still close enough to the lifeboat that I was able to grab the side and, with my other arm under Ashley's bottom, boost her up and over. I lifted myself up and in right behind her; fiery debris rained down on us as I quickly grabbed the oars and began rowing the two of us and the clay pot to safety.

If things hadn't been bad enough, I was so focused on rowing like hell for several minutes that I didn't even realize that our lifeboat was filling up with water.

CHAPTER 42:

"Austin, are we sinking?"

We were about three hundred yards from the burning ship and about eight hundred yards from the sub, and not one fellow Seal could be seen.

I wasn't about to have us try to swim toward the constantly moving sub. They had completed their mission and they were probably about ready to submerge and be on their way. If we even had a remote chance of catching up, they would not see us and the turbulent water would pull us under.

I'm sure there was absolutely no concern on board the sub for our safely, and why should there be? They had left me floating alone in a dinghy in the middle of the Atlantic Ocean with a beautiful girl awaiting the arrival of a British Navy recover vessel; they were probably envious.

It was apparent were sinking. Ashley was bailing water with her hands as fast as she could while I tried to find and repair the hole. The problem was it wasn't just a hole, the entire wood lifeboat was rotten, and water was seeping in from everywhere.

We were about ready to acquaint ourselves with the cold North Atlantic waters as the submarine was becoming smaller and smaller on the horizon as it left the scene. We could now only hope that we could tread water long enough until the Brits could arrive—not to mention how long we could fight off hypothermia or sharks.

Ashley again clutched the pot between her legs. The boat that for a brief time ferried us to freedom was now separating our company and departing to its final destination, the bottom of the sea.

"Let go of the urn, Ashley! It's too heavy it will pull us down like a rock."

"I can't. You don't understand, Austin; it's up to me to return this to its intended sepulcher."

She went under immediately. As I had predicted, the weight was too much. I caught her arm and pulled her to the surface. It would be all I could do, even with all my aquatic survival training, to keep both of us and the urn afloat for very long. I was able to collect an oar before it got away. The oars were the only part of the lifeboat that didn't sink, and it did provide some buoyancy, which did help us tread water.

Three or four hours of fighting to keep our heads above water went by, and Ashley was tiring tremendously. With the additional weight of the clay urn and its contents, the oar did not keep us afloat by itself; we had to tread our legs constantly to keep our heads above water.

I stopped pleading with her to let go of the urn, knowing that soon I would physically need to release her grip in order to keep us both from drowning. The swells were increasing, with the occasional wave breaking over us, delivering an excruciating blow. God bless Ashley. She never gave up; she kept fighting, even though her energy was almost gone. I too was exhausted, not only from keeping myself up, but holding up Ashley, who was cradling the urn. Because of my diminishing strength I feared that now one of these waves might pull her away from my clutches. The time had come; I had to pry her fingers away from the weight that threatened pulling us to our doom.

"Please, Austin," muttered Ashley as I started to unclench her fingers. Her closed eyes opened to stare into mine, as if to continue to do her pleading. Her eyes suddenly opened wider as if she was surprised by something behind me. Fearing she spotted a shark, I turned around, accidentally releasing my grip on her. She went down like a rock. Realizing what I had done, I quickly turned back around and dove under.

I had her, snatching her about six feet below the surface. She still had the urn securely in her grip, but with her free hand I pulled her to the surface.

When we arrived at the surface we were greeted by what Ashley had seen just before I let her go, and it wasn't a shark.

CHAPTER 43:

Our ship had indeed arrived, and it wasn't the British Navy. Hell, it wasn't even my U.S. Navy. Our rescue vessel was a thirty-foot wooden sailing sloop, and the hand that extended over the side and down to the water to collect us belonged to none other than the man who in Ashley's own words "has always been there for her and her family their entire life and always when they needed him the most."

"Latch on to my hand now. lassie, I'll get ya!"

Calvin gripped Ashley's wrist and pulled her as I pushed. When her butt was safely under the lifelines I lifted up the urn to him. Finally it was my turn, and once my feet finally touched the teak lattice floor of that old yacht, I gave that Irishman the biggest hug ever. I even gave him a kiss on top of his red head.

I helped a weak but happy Ashley down the steps of the companionway into the cabin below. There Calvin gave us towels and blankets. Ash slipped out of her wet clothes, then wrapped up in the blanket and collapsed in a nearby berth, where she slept for several hours.

Calvin methodically examined the outside of the clay urn with total wonderment before even touching it. Then with deliberate consternation he picked up the container of the holy tears of Mary as if was a communion scepter and carried it below, placing it on the forward berth.

Calvin reappeared through the companionway holding a cup of hot Irish coffee and handed it to me as he sat down.

"Did yah see them. lad?"

"You mean the diamonds. Calvin?"

"Yes, are they truly as beautiful as has been told?"

"Oh yes, maybe even more."

"You are a lucky man, Austin Brock!"

I smiled and nodded back at him.

"Calvin, I only have one question. How in the world did you find us? We could have been anywhere land or sea."

A mutual friend guided me here, laddie, and if we don't hurry and return the tears of Mary to Saint Patrick's tomb, our mutual friend Abraham might summon up a storm."

His wink was my signal to help hoist the canvas sails. With the wind off our beam we were on our way.

Incidentally, about a mile after we were underway, we passed a British frigate steaming toward the burning trawler. *Nice timing,* I thought to myself. *Oh well. They will have a fun time recovering the plutonium from Davy Jones's locker.*

I had one more visit from Abraham; well, it was more like a vision. Along with Ash, I had fallen asleep, but instead of being underneath in a cozy bunk, I was outside sitting under the boom in the cockpit.

It was the weirdest thing—or I should say just another weird thing in a long line of weird things that has occurred over the last several weeks, but I must have lost consciousness as soon as I wrapped myself up in the blanket that Calvin gave me, just like Ashley. That may not sound that strange, especially for someone who had been treading water and holding up a hundred-pound girl along with a forty-pound pot of diamonds and for almost four hours. However, I am a Navy Seal and have trained for conditions such as this, and I don't just fall asleep that fast and that soundly. But that was just part of this little adventure; I was awakened by someone shaking me. When I opened my eyes expecting to see Calvin or Ashley. I saw instead that familiar white-robed and silver-haired friend of mine. I wanted to thank him for leading Calvin to us, but I was unable to produce any words when I tried to speak. Abraham just smiled and in a kind and mellow voice said "Take this small gift as a token of appreciation and share it with someone special that you love. Mind that the brilliance radiated by this gift will be a barometer of the amount of love that surrounds it."

Abraham's words and silhouette faded and were replaced with the sensation of being shaken again; this time when I opened my eyes it was Calvin.

"Are ye gonna sleep for twenty years, Mr. Rip Van Winkle, or are ye gonna help me moor this boat?"

Who knows how long I was out, but instead of late evening it was now early morning. I felt something damp in the palm of my hand. Unclenching my fist, I discovered a small piece of cloth. Inside was a shimmering diamond. I didn't examine it long, for Calvin was summoning me up to the bow, so I stuck the cloth-covered diamond in my pocket and went to help.

In the horizon was the hazy outline of tall buildings. Calvin confirmed it to be Dublin. I helped lower the sails, and Calvin fired up the smoky diesel. Pretty soon we were joined topside by a bright-eyed girl who gave Calvin a huge hug, then turned and ran to me, jumping into my arms. This long wet kiss was a long overdue and neither one of us was willing to end it. However, Calvin had different ideas. He parted us by going underneath and getting a cup of cold water then tossing it on us.

"Ah, blarney stones. Can't you kids wait until we are on shore, preferably out of my eyesight."

Calvin wasn't exactly a romantic, but his point was well taken. We did need to get ourselves in to shore and Ashley home. There were family and friends who were frantically waiting for news on Ashley, as well as American and British agencies interested in the fate of the diamonds and plutonium.

We left the sea, dropping the sails, and began motoring the sloop toward the mouth of a river, cruising for several minutes up the river, then eventually turning into a cove. I spotted a mooring ahead with a dinghy attached; Calvin aimed the boat directly toward the floating target. With skillful yachtsmanship from the Irish skipper and careful instructions delivered, we hooked the floating mooring line with a pole and tied it securely to the bow. Calvin killed the engine.

We rowed the dinghy to shore, and as soon as we heard the abrasive grating of sand on the bottom of the small boat, Ashley jumped out and ran ahead. There was a tiny brown-sand beach that we used as our port; barren of any other inhabitants or dinghies but not far from civilization. Instinctively Ashley followed a stone path over a hill; on the other side was a bustling street full of fish markets merchant marine shops.

I knew I had to hurry to catch Ashley, so I left Calvin to tend to the dinghy and chased out after her. She weaved in and out of pedestrian traffic until spotting a café. Then she darted inside. By the time I arrived at the door and went inside she was already on the pay phone hanging on the wall at the back of the room.

I waved at Ashley to let her know I knew where she was, then gestured to her that I was heading back to get Calvin. With tear-filled eyes and a phone up to her ear, she smiled and nodded.

An empty dinghy was all that I found at the sandy shore. Still moored out about three hundred feet was the wooded sloop, clueing me he probably wasn't out there either.

My mission was almost complete; however, Calvin still had work to do: returning the tears of Mary to Saint Patrick's tomb.

Looking back, it was interesting that there was a changing of the guard, so to speak, in regard to the custodianship of the diamonds. Ashley took extreme care as guardian, but once she boarded the sailboat all physical stewardship immediately became Calvin's; however, I believe the spiritual steward was and has always been Abraham.

I rejoined Ashley at the café; we ate breakfast and awaited the arrival of her family.

The familiar O'Shea touring car pulled up to the curb out front. The doors flew open and Katherine was out before the car came to a complete stop. Ashley knocked over her chair as she jumped up and ran outside, and the entire O'Shea clan swarmed her outside on the sidewalk.

Two sedans full of agents pulled up across the street. Mixed in the bunch were CIA agents Kenny and Boomer King, along with British agent Smyth, hobbling on crutches.

After the customary greetings, I got back in one of the sedans with Kenny and Smyth to give them their highly anticipated debriefing. They obviously were aware of the burning trawler's coordinates from both U.S. and British naval reports, so I told them the plutonium was tossed overboard by Johnson and that if the recovery team hurried it might even find her remains still clutching the handles of one of the crates. When asked about the whereabouts of the diamonds, I told them they were on the ocean floor as well. Explaining Calvin and how he found us and how we made it safely back to shore was not so easy to do.

CHAPTER 44:

I returned to Ireland with my wife almost three years to the day after our dinghy scratched the shore of that deserted beach in Dublin. I had finished my commitment to the navy and was starting my new job, working for my father-in-law as his new sales executive. Part of training was learning everything there is to know about potatoes. It wasn't exactly going to provide the same rush as my former job, but actually I was looking forward to slowing down my life. I'd had more than my share of adrenaline-charged adventures in a relatively short period of time and was actually excited at the anticipation of opening a new office back in the States, maybe even in Indiana.

One of the first things we wanted to do while back was visit Bryan. It was a coincidence that he was also returning home to check on his bed and breakfast. He'd left a friend to manage it while he was away for his new employment. It seemed British Intelligence was so impressed by his heroics at Saint Patrick's grave that as soon as his wounds healed they offered him a low-level job at MI-Six. Bryan was living his dream and I fully expect him to shoot up the ladder there—well, at least until someone discovers his past involvement with the IRA.

We were not doing anything, however, until we returned to my most favorite place in Ireland, and that was the spot where I proposed to my love. I will always remember that day.

Heeding Abraham's advice, I had that diamond set into a gold engagement ring and was ready to present it along with my proposal, but I needed to do something first. I felt compelled to do the right thing by asking her brother, who had also been my close friend, for his forgiveness and permission to marry his younger sis. It was a hard thing for me to do, but when I said my piece I felt a burden was lifted off my chest. I actually felt some closure. Perhaps indeed I was forgiven.

I stood up from kneeling at Tommy's grave and turned to Ashley, only to re-kneel on my other knee and present her the ring and ask her to share the rest of her life with me. To my surprise she also had a gift for me as well. Digging deep in her purse, she pulled out a little black box and opened it; it seemed she was also visited by Abraham; her diamond was still wrapped in cloth, as it was given to her.

"I was told to share this with the one I love," cried Ashley. "I thought I was dreaming but when I awoke this was in the palm of my hand. Austin, you are the one I love."

The O'Shea family cemetery was situated on a large hill overlooking their castle and the surrounding lush meadows. We both sat at the foot of Tommy's grave watching the sunset and playing with the new addition to our family, a black Labrador retriever we named Keller.

Today the sunset was as gorgeous as it was a few years ago, the day when I proposed to Ashley. I didn't want to leave this view and the warm feeling I felt inside. I was looking at an angel as Ashley's beautiful auburn hair was now being highlighted by the amber glow of the sun. She sat motionless, staring at the solar orb, her elbows on her knees with her hands cupped around her chin. It was hard to distinguish between the sparkle of her deep blue eyes and Mary Magdalene's tear on her finger. For this brief moment in time, I felt as if I couldn't get any closer to heaven.

Well, the time had come for us to leave this wonderful place. Katherine was expecting us for dinner and would not accept any excuses for tardiness.

Ashley took a hold of my hand and lifted both of our arms up and extended them out as if we had the palms of our hands on top of the sun. This gave the illusion that the last fleeting seconds of sun sinking into the Earth were controlled by us.

I believe that God has a purpose for all of us. It's as certain as the sun setting in the horizon. I also believe that each one of us has the ability to control our own destiny by simply listening to our heart.

Go live life, and listen to your heart.

THE END

ABOUT THE AUTHOR

I, too, am a typical Indiana country boy. I attribute a lot of my creative imagination from being raised in the country. I spent many of my childhood days playing in the corn fields and wooded ravines which surrounded my home pretending to be a cowboy, fighting Indians or an Army man, trying to recapture a hill from the enemy.

Today I live in the suburbs outside of Indianapolis, Indiana. Between my beautiful wife and I, we have four wonderful kids; one mine, two hers, and one ours.

When I'm not at the office Monday through Friday doing my daytime job (vice president of a large construction company), you will find me at the gym working out; attending my youngest son's tae kwon do. basketball events or in front of the computer writing.

If you ask anyone who knows me, they will tell you that my true passion is sailing. Sailing is not an activity, it's an expression of art.It's caputuring one of nature's elements (wind) momentarily to cause a reaction to an inanimate object (boat). If you don't know what I'm talking about, you have never experienced the beauty of sailing.

Printed in the United States
100288LV00004B/88-114/A